ROBERT FLANAGAN

STORY HOUR
&
OTHER STORIES

WORKING LIVES SERIES
BOTTOM DOG PRESS

HURON, OHIO

© 2014 Robert Flanagan
& Bottom Dog Press, Inc.

ISBN 978-1-933964-77-5

Bottom Dog Publishing
PO Box 425, Huron, Ohio 44839
http://smithdocs.net
e-mail: Lsmithdog@smithdocs.net

General Editor: Larry Smith
Copy Editor: Jessica Roth
Layout & Cover Design: Susanna Sharp-Schwacke

Views and Reviews of Robert Flanagan's Fiction

"Robert Flanagan is a writer of originality and force."
—Alison Lurie

Maggot

X.J. Kennedy: "A living American classic, a book that bites and never lets go."

Ron Hansen: "*Maggot* is a great book, full of anger and power and humor and heart."

Donald Ray Pollock: "When it comes to novels written about boot camp life in the United States military, nothing compares to Robert Flanagan's revealing and wonderfully written classic, *Maggot*."

Naked to Naked Goes

Studs Terkel: "Robert Flanagan with these powerful stories joins Tobias Wolff as one of my very favorite contemporary writers."

Tim O'Brien: "What a terrific group of stories ... drama in the very best sense, all of it activated by clean, tight powerful prose. A jewel that will be shining for years to come."

Loving Power

Newsday: "The power of love in Robert Flanagan's vigorous collection of stories, set in his native Ohio, is bruising ... especially when he lets his sprightly characters speak directly in their taut Midwestern drawls. His storytelling is as solid as rock. The author of three previous works of fiction, Flanagan deserves a wider audience."

Annabel Thomas: "*Loving Power* has all the pluses readers have come to expect from Robert Flanagan's work: Superb humor. Drama done with passion, insight and honesty. Technical brilliance. Innovation. And taut, compelling prose. There is something more here as well: a remarkable plumbing of the human spirit."

Columbus *Dispatch*: "A number of stories in this collection of seven are genuinely funny. For their humor, pathos, wisdom and Flanagan's fine inventiveness with language, these are stories well worth reading."

rflanaga@columbus.rr.com   www.robertflanagan.com

ALSO BY ROBERT FLANAGAN

FICTION

Maggot, a novel, 1971, 2nd Ed. 2012
Three Times Three, stories, 1977
Naked to Naked Goes, stories, 1986
Loving Power, stories, 1989
Fight Night, stories, 2011

POETRY

Not for Dietrich Bonhoeffer, 1969
The Full Round, 1973
Once You Learn You Never Forget, 1978
Reply to an Eviction Notice, 2009

PLAYS

Jupus Redeye, 1988

TABLE OF CONTENTS

STORY HOUR

On his way out of the library's community room amid the stream of parents and grandparents, women, mostly, with children hanging on them or racing ahead with their books to the check-out counter, Virgel was asked by Miss Julie, the children's librarian, if she might speak with him for a moment. He nodded and cleared the aisle to stand between her desk and the tropical fish tank. Children were not allowed to touch the tank, but it was a real job to keep them from doing it. Quentin and Noel always wanted to tap on the glass to get the fishies' attention.

The Jamaican lady from story hour, Aurelia, gave him a smile as she passed by with her granddaughter Yolanda in tow. Virgel could not recall ever having met anyone with teeth as white as hers. Like those little marshmallows his grandsons loved in their hot chocolate.

Miss Julie was a tall, stringy woman, young, early thirties, smiling and friendly, who wore snug jeans and fluffy white blouses and, surprisingly, bore a blue tattoo of a snake on her right forearm. Surprising to Virgel, anyway, but then he was an old fart and out of touch with current fashion. Although as his wife Emma would have said, bless her heart, there never was a time when he'd been *in* fashion. Overalls at home, washable khakis and plaid flannel shirts for town: that was his wardrobe for as long as she had known him. Thirty-eight years, seven months, nine days. Passed more than two years now, Emma was. God forgive him, but he wished he had been the first to go.

"I didn't see Noel today," Miss Julie said. "Is he sick?"

"Nope, healthy as a horse."

"Then why wasn't he ..."

"Kindergarten. Started yesterday and loves it already. Claims he's the best reader in the class and I believe him. You folks can take a lot of the credit for that. Same with Quentin, our first grader. Every week they've hauled home an armload of books, and their mother reads to them every night."

Miss Julie glanced down at the desk. "Mister Dodd ..." She looked back up, her face coloring, her eyes rolling up somewhere over his head.

Lord, he hoped she wasn't having a heart attack. He'd passed his Heimlich maneuver class at the Senior Citizens Center last year but had never used it on anyone but the dummy.

"People don't attend story hour without children," she said.

"Well, no, I can see why. But there's no rule against it, is there?"

Now she met his look. "In fact, there is."

"Oh."

"It might make some of the mothers ... to have a man there by himself. You understand I'm sure."

Virgel felt his own face turning red as a beet.

"Nobody ever said anything—but, well, sure, I see what you're saying. I kinda wish somebody would have said something earlier. You ought to put up a sign."

"This is first time the issue's come up, but thank you. I'll pass your suggestion on to our director."

Looking at his feet, he said he was sorry to have caused any—

"Mr. Dodd, please. No need to apologize. We all know you would never ... But that's the policy. I'm sure you understand."

"All right."

He walked quickly to the lobby. As a rule he would stop by the circulation desk to browse the rack of damaged or out of fashion books on sale for a dollar each or six for five dollars, where his would buy six at a time to have handy on nights he couldn't sleep. When he had read the good ones and given up on the rest, he would return the lot to the library so they could sell them again. But, now he passed by the rack, shouldered through the front doors, crossed the parking lot and fired up his Buick.

By rights, he ought to go back and apologize to the librarian for that "put up a sign" remark. Just because a man was a fool didn't mean he had to be petty. Another thing he could tell her was that he wasn't simpleminded. Fact is, he hadn't noticed any single men there, but then he didn't come to story hour to gawk at the other adults. He was there for his grandchildren and paid attention to them. Just like the Jamaican lady paid attention to hers. They didn't work on their laptops, read their Kindles or take catnaps like a lot of the others, people there just to dump their kids on the library for an hour.

Truth to tell, he liked listening to a woman's voice reading children's stories and reciting Mother Goose. He couldn't recall his mother reading him Mother Goose, though maybe she had when he was too young to remember or maybe now he was getting senile and forgetful, though if that was his problem how could he know for sure?

But one thing he knew for a fact: he was no pervert.

Quentin and Noel had both loved to cuddle on grandpa's lap and hear him recite those great old rhymes.

His heart racing, he took slow deep breaths, in and out, in and out, as his doctor had told him to do.

All right then. He'd go apologize to the tattooed girl.

But not today.

He backed his old Buick LeSabre out of its slot and aimed at the exit.

At the Dunkin Donuts shop he bought six chocolate chip cookies, an apple fritter and a medium black coffee with two sugars, and then drove across town to Emily's condo. He parked in a visitor's space and carried the bag and coffee to the door without dropping or spilling anything. Hands full, he kicked at the door, which he knew she didn't like, but what else could he do with his hands full, yell for her? That would be even worse, the way she liked things quiet.

She opened the door—not using the chain lock as he had warned her to do—pressed the button to check if the doorbell wasn't working, said for him to come in, and then went to sit at her computer.

He leaned back against the door shutting it tight, then stepped into the small dining room and set the cookie bag on the table—cherry veneer it looked like—that matched the five-shelf glassed cabinet packed with books. He was glad to see that the reading habit she'd learned at home was still with her, that it wasn't all just computer and those electronic books.

Nowadays everywhere you looked people were on laptops, cell phones, and those computer book readers. At Bob Evans he had sat at a table across from a man and a woman in a booth, and all through their lunch they talked to other people on their cell phones and said not one word to each other. And now, there even was a phone you stuck in your ear. Waiting to cross the street in Olentangy a couple of months past, he stood next to a fellow in a business suit who started talking a mile a minute. Virgel said "What?" but the man acted like he wasn't even there. Nobody else was there either, and Virgel backed away, thinking it best to steer clear of folks with voices in their heads.

In the living room Virgel took off his coat and lowered himself onto a platform rocker, taking care to hold his cup level and not spill any coffee.

"Just a sec," his daughter Emily said, tapping keys.

He nodded. Himself, he couldn't think of anything much worse than staring at a computer all day, but when he'd tried to sympathize with her about it, Em claimed it was a great job transcribing medical records for doctors and clinics, making good money from home. That was why she'd taken all those online courses. Didn't he remember?

Suddenly, she spun about on her stool. "I can't stand this," she groaned "It's slow! And it's not just me, either. Craig worked on it, trying to speed it up, but ... When he gets home we'll need to shop for a new one, program or computer."

"Must be kinda hard having him on the road so much."

"He's in sales, Dad. He has to be."

Virgel nodded. There were chocolate chip cookies in the bag there, he said.

"Thank you."

Would she like him to get her one?

"Not right now. I'm so ... Besides, I'm on a diet."

"I can't see where you need to lose."

"But I do."

He sipped his coffee as she glanced back at the computer screen. Without looking away, she asked Virgel what he was up to today.

"Nothing much. Just thought I'd drop by."

"Well, thank you," she said, standing. "But I really wish ..."

He lurched to his feet. "I know, I know. You're on the clock. Must be kinda tough working at home."

"Not at all. I save a commute and I can pick up the boys from school. It's a good arrangement actually."

"I suppose. Just seems it'd be pretty hard to relax when the work's right there waitin' on you."

"Like a farmer on his farm?"

"Well now, that's a whole different ..."

She slipped past him to open the door. "I mentioned the possibility of you getting a dog, remember? They're good company and walking them is good exercise."

"No, not in an apartment."

"They're not allowed? You asked?"

Virgel shook his head. "It's only common sense."

Emily nodded. "I need to get back to work."

"Those ducks look pretty good in there."

"Don't they? Craig likes them, too."

"Glad to hear it. Well ..." He backed out of the doorway.

"I appreciate you thinking of me, Dad. Really I do."

Virgel spent the rest of the week giving his apartment a good cleaning, getting down on his hands and knees to scrub the floors and washing and drying his bedding in the basement laundry room after Lord knows how long. At home Emma had insisted on doing the linen once a month and, come summer, hanging it out on the line so it smelled of fresh air.

He went to the discount center and bought the boys cowboy hats, both red so they wouldn't have cause to fight over them.

As he parked in his slot at home, he spotted the gaunt old lady who called herself Lizbeth walking that yappy, ugly little fuzzball she claimed was a pedigree something called a cockapoo, of all things. She passed him by as if he were invisible.

Virgel shrugged it off. He did appreciate her having invited him in for tea that time but didn't regret that he wasn't about to get a repeat invite. Not that he hadn't been impressed by her apartment: spic and span and all polished wood and dim lights in fringed parchment shades, with scratchy but kind of pretty violin music coming from a stereo. Tea was served in the tiny dining room on her very best English china: Lemon Rose herbal tea and Madeleine cookies which were precisely what your better class in England preferred. Virgel was impressed and said so, but during tea she went on and on complaining about their neighbors and how humiliating it was for her that due to her reduced financial circumstances she was forced to associate with such uncouth louts. The moment he got the chance, Virgel had made for the door.

Emily didn't call him for over a week. He thought of calling her, but thought again. He didn't want to make a pest of himself. He'd made it clear that he was willing to take the boys for an hour or so whenever she needed a break, but he guessed that now they were so busy with school she didn't get much time with them herself and so didn't need his help.

Weeks later at the Coffee Cup on Main Street, Virgel straddled a stool at the diner's U-shaped back counter. Without story hour as part of his day, he'd taken to eating a late breakfast with the ten o'clock bunch every day of the week except Sundays, when he treated himself to lunch at Bob Evans.

Finishing his fritter, he took a refill on coffee and looked at the house copy of the *Sentinel* to see if anything important was going on and if anybody he knew had died. About the only "news" was that City Council was talking about hiring a city manager, though they hadn't voted on it yet.

The weekly notices of the County Sheriff's sales of properties of owners delinquent on their mortgages took up a twelve pages of tiny print now, half the twenty-four page, bigger print issue. Every Monday the paper ran such notices.

Virgel flapped the paper at the others. What he failed to understand, he said, was how the bankers and politicians could keep throwing people out of their homes. Where the heck were they supposed to go? Who was going to buy up all those empty houses? What the County Sheriff ought to be doing was to catch those Cleveland drug dealers driving through Olentangy on their way to Columbus and leave honest folks' homes alone.

"You don't pay your way," Pat Monahan, said, "you don't get to stay."

Virgel passed the paper on down the counter. The whole business made his blood boil, and he breathed slowly like his doctor had told him to do.

The real shame, Monahan, a big-mouth real estate hotshot, said was that the local market was way down. No mystery about it neither. "This county's going all to hell. No offense to you, Willis, but fact is we let a low class of Columbus nigger take over the south side, and now you got your A-rabs and Spics moving in to the east. Won't be long before your natural born white Americans will be a minority in this county."

Willis, who ran Tick Tock Clock Repair and Sales and pitched no-hitters for the Odd Fellows softball team, just shook his head. A couple of mossbacks grunted, maybe agreeing, maybe not. Most everyone else scraped at his plate or stirred his coffee. Nobody there much liked Monahan, a know-it-all known to screw people who bought houses from him.

"Ever read a book, Pat?" Virgel asked Monahan.

"What?"

"Book?" Virgel spread clasped palms as if opening a book. "County Library over by the Courthouse there has stacks of them."

"I knew you were dumb, Dodd," Monahan said, "but not *that* dumb."

Grinning, he looked around at the others, but none of them gave him much notice.

"One of them that I read," Virgel said, "told all about the Irish coming to America back in the 1840's potato famine. Dirt-poor Catholic farmers couldn't read nor write nor hardly speak a word of English and they brought litters of dirty kids with them. Know what 'Americans' called them, Pat Monahan? 'The niggers of Europe.'"

Virgel took a sip of coffee.

Across the counter Monahan stood, looking like he'd like to box Virgel's ears for him. But then he shrugged.

"I don't have time for this happy horseshit. You all may be retarded," (what he always called the retired guys though it never got a laugh) "but I've got business to see to." He clattered a quarter on the counter, and walked out.

Maggie brought around the coffee pot, refilling any cup without a hand over it.

Charlie Gibson, a plumber, looked up from the *Sentinel* and asked what in heck did Olentangy need a city manager for? Mayors had done all right for a hundred years, hadn't they?

Willis thought maybe it could save some tax money.

"Hell, anything new always costs more," somebody said.

Gibson slapped the counter. "Change for the sake of change, that's all it is!"

On the three and a half miles back to his apartment, Virgel drove nine point three miles out of his way, as he often did, to loop out around their old farm house. It galled him to see how the new people there were letting the place run down. A loose gutter hung down across the window of the back east side bedroom window, the one he and Emma had shared. There were weeds where Emma's daylilies and hostas once grew and the front porch where Virgel used to sit and whittle looked to be missing a board or two. He had a mind to stop and have a word with the people, but they'd just tell him it wasn't his place any-more and to get off their property or they'd call the sheriff. Well, to hell with them then. They could ruin the place but they couldn't ruin Virgel's memories of it.

Climbing the stairs to his apartment he heard his phone ringing and fumbled with his keys to unlock the door, but before he managed it the ringing stopped. He checked the recorder Emily had talked him into buying, but no message light showed. He started to call her back, but stopped. If it was important she would have left him a message. And more than a few times, the message had been not to call her because she'd be taking a nap.

He sat in his rocker to steady his breathing and rest his eyes for a minute. When the phone rang again it snapped him out of a doze and he stumbled up to seize the receiver.

"Em?"

"Excuse me. Is this Virgeel?"

"I'm here."

"Are you all right?"

"Who is this?"

"I am sorry if I wake you. I am the lady from the library."

"From the—Oh, Aurelia?"

"Yes. If this is a bad time ..."

"No, no. I thought you were my daughter. Are things okay?"

"Yes, but we do not see you at story hour now two weeks and I am worried."

"I'm fine," he told her, free hand clutching his crotch. "Grownups can't come to story hour without kids."

"Ohhh. Yes, of course."

Hopping from foot to foot, he said "Sorry, but I ... think my daughter is trying to reach me."

"Goodbye."

Leaving the receiver off the hook, Virgel hot-footed it to the bathroom, threw up the seat and released his bursting bladder just in the nick of time.

Evenings, he had taken to sitting out back of his apartment on a kitchen chair, beside him a paper sack holding the short ends of 2X4s he picked up for nothing from the scrap barrel at the Farmer's Exchange lumber yard. Sitting outside whittling was a thing he'd enjoyed most all his life.

Emma had liked to call him her woodcarver, bragging to her lady friends about his artistic talent, though that was far from the truth. A wood carver, he tried telling her, used all sort of tools: chisels, gouges, draw knives, mallets, a vise, maybe even an adze. Virgel was just a whittler, using an old two-bladed pocket knife, a boy's knife really, and making things like whistles, a kerchief ring, small bowls, and those lumpy ducks she kept on display in about every room in the house.

Well, it was wood carving to her.

One of things he and Emma loved, besides each other, was wood. When she was upset about something, nothing eased her mind like a walk in the patch of woods just beyond the pasture. The thick roots and leafy shade there most always had the power to lift her spirits. And Virgel, when he sat outside and whittled, felt pretty much the same. Wood was a natural and solid thing you had to have for your house and furniture, but also something that just looking at could make you feel good.

Their Em, though, had never taken to the woods, too gloomy. But she had liked long walks in the fields with Sparky, a little mongrel stray that stuck to her like glue until it got run over by their neighbor Clyde Jackson's three-point disc harrow.

Still, it seemed to Virgel that Em was happy enough back then. What her problem was now he had no idea. He supposed that was what came of marrying the wrong man. Though no doubt she'd deny it, Em, or Emily as she wanted to be called now, more than likely was touchy because she was so worried—though too proud to admit it—that she maybe was losing her man. All those old traveling salesman jokes didn't just come out of thin air. A man spending most of his time alone on the road wouldn't have much trouble running into a woman willing to comfort him. Or so Virgel had heard.

Though, truth to tell, Em always had been the nervous sort, just a natural-born worrier. Her second year in high school, though her grades were good, she had started playing sick, not wanting to go to school. Some of the other girls teased her about her thick glasses and her homemade clothes. Emma told Em they were only jealous because their mothers didn't care enough about them to spend time sewing, but it made no difference in Em's behavior. If her folks hadn't kept after her, Virgel believed she might have been content to spend all her time staying home from school and up in her room, showing no interest whatsoever in her folks, the house, meals or chores. The little dog her father had whittled for her she had put on a shelf in her book case, back in a corner where it grew a coat of dust. Virgel would be the first to admit it didn't look very much like Sparky, but you could see it was meant to be a dog and it had cost him a chunk of his time to make it for her.

Emma had been afraid of Em becoming a drop-out and made her get up and get dressed no matter her crying and complaining. On days when Em missed the bus—purposely, according to Emma—it fell to Virgel to drive her to school, with her sulking the whole way and not saying thanks or even goodbye when he dropped her off.

Then next thing they knew the girl had joined the Liberty Baptist Church, an evangelical outfit where folks sang and clapped and flapped their arms like chicken wings and hugged each other and cried. Virgel didn't know what to make of it. The last time he had been in a church was when he and Emma got married by the Free Will Baptist preacher whose little church Emma's mother went to. And Emma had not set foot in the place since her mother's funeral there.

When they pressed Em as to why on earth she had taken up church-going, she said because it made her feel better. Virgel had to wonder just what could make her feel so bad that she had to go to church for it. He wanted to forbid her to have anything to do with those holy rollers but Emma said no, best let her go; it seemed to be something she needed and maybe could make her a bit more cheerful.

Whatever Em's problems were, she'd never let on to Virgel. And if she'd gone to her mother with them, he had a hard time believing Emma wouldn't have told him. The two of them shared everything. In fact it sometimes worried him that that was part of Em's problem. Her folks seemed so happy at home maybe she couldn't bring herself to tell them that she wasn't.

At church maybe she could let it all out. Himself, he wouldn't know.

Not that Emma and Vergil had no differences or tough times, but they hadn't let the bad times last. When Emma was upset she'd walk in the woods beyond the pasture. Trees with their heavy roots and leafy shade most always made her feel better. Virgel felt better whittling. A block of wood was something solid, a thing you could shape to your liking.

Next day at coffee club, Virgel saw in the *Sentinel* that the Humane Society had a slew of dogs and cats looking for homes. He supposed a cat wouldn't be all that much trouble at his place. At the farm Emma had tossed scraps to the barn cats that kept the rat and mouse population down, but they never let any of the feral cats and their fleas in the house. Whenever Vergil judged there were too many around the place, he'd drown the new litters in the rain barrel.

Emma's cousin Eva, who they visited once a year over to Guernsey County, kept three cats as house pets: soft, overfed things that never did a lick of work. She acted like they were her babies. Emma and Eva would chat in the parlor, each with a fat cat on her lap that looked about to spill their cups of tea. Then the leftover cat would try to climb onto Virgel's lap he'd push it off. You could see Eva didn't care for that, but that was her problem, not his. He just didn't like cats. You could see in their eyes that really they could take you or leave you. A dog now, he was loyal, was your pal. Problem was he was a messy, noisy pal—barking at most anything, waking you up in the middle of the night over nothing, chewing on your shoes and needing to be walked three times a day so he could pee on trees and have you scoop up his poop.

The Humane Society folk even had a monkey out there needing a home, though why anyone would want a monkey in the house Virgel failed to understand. They were loud, dirty creatures who were all the time jerking off. Virgel felt low enough about his own bad habit without having a caged monkey showing him how pathetic it was.

He guessed at his age he just didn't feel like putting up with the mess that pets and other folk brought into your life.

On Saturday Em and Craig wanted to go to an art exhibit at the museum in Columbus, so Virgel got to have the boys for the day. He took them to the Coffee Cup for lunch where they had fun spinning like tops on the swivel stools and eating greasy grilled cheese sandwiches and French fries and sweet rolls. You could tell by their grins they didn't get that at home.

Afterwards he took them to the library to play with the big plastic building blocks and pick out books to take home. The children's librarian was nowhere to be seen, but the head librarian gave him a friendly hello and Virgel figured he wasn't banned from the entire building, only story hour.

Leaving Quentin and Noel in the play area, telling them to stay put, he quick-stepped to the men's room to empty his bladder. Why a man had a prostate if all it did was cause him trouble, he failed to understand.

As he left the men's he was surprised to spy Aurelia at the return counter, sliding books one by one spine-first through the slot as he'd taught the boys to do. He looked around the corner to make sure that Noel and Quentin were where they were supposed to be, and approached Aurelia.

"Hi there, stranger."

She glanced up, a smile flickering briefly on her lips. "Virgeel," she said, depositing the last book.

"Mrs. Williams," a librarian said, "There's a book here for you."

"Thank you! Here is my card."

Virgel stood aside as Aurelia checked out the book.

When she finished he thought they'd have a chance to talk, but no, she turned and walked out the door, leaving him standing there numb as a stump.

"May I help you, Mister Dodd?" the librarian asked.

"No."

Mrs. *Williams*? He'd never even thought to ask her her last name.

He went back to play with the boys.

At home, he felt just awful. The last thing he wanted to do was hurt the lady's feelings. She didn't deserve that. If he knew her phone number he'd ring her up that minute. The library might have her number, but he wasn't about to ask them for it and maybe get pegged as a stalker.

The following Wednesday he drove to the library when it was about time for story hour to let out, and parked his car on down the row from Aurelia's red Camry. When folks started coming out, he opened one of his six for five dollar paperbacks as if were reading it. Spotting Yolanda pushing open the door, he got out of his car, books in hand, and started toward the outside return, then stopped. "Oh, hi there, Yolanda, Aurelia."

"Virgeel."

He lifted the handful of books. "Just dropping these off."

"I see."

"So. How are the lovely Williams ladies today?"

"We are fine, thank you," Aurelia said. "And you are well?"

"Right as rain."

She smiled and headed to her car. When he followed she stopped, half-turning. "Something you want?"

"Thought maybe I could treat you two to lunch at Bob Evans."

"You do not need ..."

"But I *want* to."

"Why?"

"Well, anymore I don't get to see you much."

Aurelia asked Yolanda if she would like to go to lunch with Mister Dodd. To Virgel's relief, the girl nodded. He offered to drive them in his car and bring them back to pick up hers, but Aurelia saw no need for that.

"But look it here." He held out a hand at his car as though introducing it. "This is a 1988 Buick LeSabre V-8. You ever see anything like it?

Aurelia nodded. Like the old cars in Cuba.

"Oh no! Excuse me, but we're not talking about some junky old taxi cab. This beauty has only 41,280 some miles on the odometer. You are looking at an

American classic. There's no telling how much folks would pay to have it, but whatever it is don't matter because I'm not selling. Riding in this is like floating on a cloud."

Aurelia smiled broadly. "Really?"

"Come on, get in."

"Thank you, but no. We will meet you there."

"Okay." He swung open his driver's door and hunched to get in.

"Are you forgetting to return your books"

"Oh, right." He straightened up. "No sense risking a fine."

At Bob Evans, Virgel danced his index and middle fingers on Yolanda's place mat, quietly singing "Dance any way that you want to, dance any way you please, dance any way that you want to, but stop when I say *freeze!*" His frozen fingers ended up with one high in the air and the other nearly falling over sideways; Yolanda's hung upside down in mid-leap higher than her head.

Sandy, one of his favorite waitresses, took their orders and asked Mr. Dodd how he was feeling. Fine, just fine, he told her, enjoying the day with his good friends Mrs. Williams and her lovely daughter Yolanda.

As they ate, Virgel confessed to Aurelia that he kind of missed story hour. He guessed that over the past four, five years bringing the boys he'd come to look forward to it, and this year had come to enjoy Aurelia and Yolanda being there. But things changed, he knew that. That was the way life went.

When Sandy dropped off the bill Aurelia offered to split it, but he shook his head. His treat, remember?

"Thank you," she said. "I will leave the tip."

He bit back the "no" on his lips. "Thanks."

"You're welcome." She folded two singles under a water glass. And, she added, if Virgel wished, he might come to story hour with them so he would not be a man alone. That was awfully kind of her, he said. He might just take her up on it.

The next day he sat on a bench in the library's front lobby leafing through a book of photographs of the great Ohio flood of 1913, the worst weather disaster in

Ohio history, the whole state getting 6 to 11 inches of rain, 40,000 homes flooded and 467 people dead. Virgel shook his head. What a terrible thing that must have been. Here you were, thinking yourself safe and dry at home, out of that awful downpour, and next thing you knew your house was off its foundation and heading down the river like a Creole Queen paddle wheeler on the Mississippi, your dead chickens afloat, your cows and horses swimming for their lives.

When Aurelia showed up, she gave him a smile, saying that he must be a fast reader if he was there so soon to borrow more books.

No, he told her, just waiting to go to story hour with them.

"Yolanda, isn't that nice? Mister Dodd will be joining us."

The following week she invited him over for an authentic Jamaican meal, and he showed up on the dot, carrying a bottle of Chablis and a bouquet of purple mums from the supermarket.

She thanked him warmly and ushered him into her place, a really nice condo that would make two of his apartment. He told her how beautiful it was and said he wouldn't even ask how much rent she paid.

"Is nothing," she said. "I own it."

"You do?" He shook his head in wonder. "Not to be nosey, but ..."

"My father was a rich man."

"Well, aren't you the lucky lady."

She shrugged her shoulders, her head angled to one side.

"I mean I sure would like having more to hand down to Em when I'm gone, but the farm never did make all that much."

"But you gave her something more valuable. Your name."

"My name? Well, sure."

"Because you married her mother. Made her feel belonged. Of value."

"Right," he said, glancing down at his plate, but then forcing himself to look up, meeting her moist eyes. "I know that's real important to a girl. Boys, too, I guess. Knowing their father loves them, that he's proud of them."

"Yes," Aurelia said, and then told him to sit.

Although he'd been a bit worried about eating Jamaican food, Virgel found himself enjoying it all; cream of pumpkin soup, ackee and salt fish, and brown sugar pastries filled with jellied coconut.

"Now, *that* was a fine meal," he told her.

She thanked him and made him stay seated as she cleared the table. She returned from the kitchen with two small glasses and a bottle of rum.

He cupped a hand over his glass before she could pour. Thank you, but not for him.

He did not like Jamaican rum?

That wasn't it. He'd just never taken to drinking alcohol.

Wasn't he a man of surprises!

Not that he wanted to seem ungrateful.

Not at all. Lifting her glass, she offered a toast to his health and happiness. And later, as he was leaving, surprised him with a peck on the cheek just before closing the door.

He waited two days before calling her to ask if he could meet them at story hour again. The first few times he called and, when no one answered, he hung up, but the third time he left a message. Getting no reply that day and all the next, he drove over in the evening to check if things were all right. No one answered the door. The next day when he checked and got the same result, he knocked at a neighbor's door, telling the lady that he was friend of Mrs. Williams and was wondering if she was all right.

As far as the neighbor knew she was. She'd gone to Cleveland, something to do with family.

For how long?

That, she didn't know.

Virgel thanked her and clumped back down the stairs.

Why hadn't she called him or at least left him a note? Had he disappointed her somehow? Had that smooch on the cheek been a kiss-off for being such a wet blanket? What kind of ungrateful bumpkin refused to share a drink with a lady?

Well, hell, he'd never claimed to be some slicker.

He stewed about the woman's disappearance the rest of that week, having so much trouble sleeping that he thought maybe he ought to just take a couple of shots of rye nights. But he didn't. No sense adding another bad habit to his list.

He had made up his mind to forget about her— that he was only making a fool of himself, that there was nothing worse than an old fool and that he'd been getting along just fine before he met her and could do just fine without her if that was the way it was to be, before she phoned him.

When he showed up at her condo, he brought along one of his whittled ducks as a gift. Aurelia was delighted to accept it, saying she loved folk art.

As they sat in her roomy living room, she in the love seat, he in an armchair, she told him her daughter had had to move to Cleveland for her job with only one week's notice, which she thought was shameful, her company treating her like she was no more than field slave, although to be truthful the job paid quite well and they also paid her moving expenses. But Aurelia would miss Yolanda so.

She figured on moving there, too?

No, she did not think so. She had helped Jessica and Yolanda to get settled there, pointing out the advantages that a big city would have for a young professional woman: new friends, more places to go. Promising to visit them every month. But she herself had no desire to live in a big city.

Virgel said he was happy to hear that.

"Are you?"

"Sure. I like it here."

"That, I know."

Virgel nodded. "So what sort of job does your daughter's husband have?"

"Job? Please. He could not take a *job*. He is a genius! A flamenco guitarist so good he has little need to practice. So especial he cannot accept any work short of concert hall engagements. After their divorce Jessica was forced to go to the courts to get child support. The judge, she did not care one bit about the genius's music career. No, she told him that if he did not wish to go to jail, then he must pay his fair share every month even if he had to take a job like others adults. Now he pays his fair share, but not out of love, only out of fear."

"That's sort of sad."

"Even a simple peasant knows if you sow the seed you must tend it if it is to grow into a healthy plant."

"An old farmer like me knows that, too."

"Yes. You are a good man."

"Well, I don't—I mean, thank you."

"You are welcome."

"And, if you don't mind my asking, what about your husband?"

"My husband?" She laughed. "I have no husband. I did not wish to have one. Jamaican men treat their women like whores and washer women."

Virgel looked at his shoes. "Sorry."

"I am not offended. I am proud to say it was my choice."

Virgel nodded. "Good for you."

"Thank you. You will stay for dinner?"

"If I'm welcome."

Come morning he was up at dawn. Not that he was too embarrassed to stay in bed with her after last night, he didn't think, just that after a lifetime of rising at cock crow it was his natural habit.

The coffee pot on the kitchen counter was some sort of space-age silver and black thing with rows of buttons. In one of the cupboards he found a silvery bag of Jamaican Blue Mountain coffee beans that looked pretty expensive, but he didn't want to use the grinder and wake her up. And if there was any instant, he couldn't find it. He ran himself a glass of tap water and sat on a black wire chair at a little round table with a glossy red top.

What to make of things now, he didn't know. He sort of wanted to skedaddle while Aurelia was asleep, but worried it might hurt her feelings. But it was going to be hard to sit there talking with her like nothing had happened. He shook his head in wonder. He'd had no idea just how beautiful she was, how smooth her skin, how firm her breasts, how full her bottom. Not that the last had surprised him. To tell the truth, it wasn't only her big white smile that had first attracted him. He had always admired a woman with an ample back porch. Like Emma's.

If the God-believers were right, was Emma looking down on him from heaven right now? If she was, how was she feeling? Upset that he had slept with another woman? Or, big-hearted as always, happy for him that he had found company?

"You are up early," Aurelia said, smiling.

"Oh. Sure. Good morning."

She leaned against the wall in the kitchen doorway.

"Farmers, you know."

"Early riser, is that the saying?"

"Up with the roosters," he said, unable to tear his eyes from the clingy gown she wore with probably nothing at all underneath.

Aurelia went to the counter, ground beans and started the coffee maker. Waiting for the pot to fill, she stepped behind him and massaged his shoulders, her full breasts touching the back of his head and making his shorts uncomfortably snug.

She filled two white mugs with the strong dark brew.

Not looking up, Virgel said he was sorry about last night, the way he disappointed her, and that—

Reaching across the table she placed a finger on his lips.

It was all right. She understood.

Because he was real grateful and—

"Stop," she told him.

No, now, he wanted to get it out. He was grateful to her for making him feel ... love again. But last night? He didn't know. Maybe he was too excited, or could be he was just out of practice.

She laughed, but when he looked hurt, stopped and took his hand in hers. Everything was all right. Truthfully. He was a good man.

Well, he didn't know about that.

And she wanted him in her life.

She did?

"Yes."

"You mean get married?"

"No."

"How come?"

"It is not something I believe in."

"But ..."

"No. That is just the way I am."

When he left, he felt—he wasn't sure just what. Not ashamed. Better in a way. But worried some about how Em would take it. Though for all he knew, she'd be fine with it. Let him get in someone else's hair for a change.

Maybe he felt a bit scared, too. But overall, he thought, he felt *excited*. A way he hadn't felt for quite a while and that might take some getting used to. However things went, it had to be better than just trying to get through another day, driving around eating fritters and wondering where the heck his life had gone.

For their third month "anniversary" he treated Aurelia to Sunday brunch, driving them in his classic Buick to Worthington to eat at the Inn there. A fancy historical place that went all the way back to the Victorian age, he told her, which had been a heck of a long time ago.

On the drive back to Olentangy she laid a hand across the back of the seat and rubbed his neck.

To his way of thinking, he said, they were a pretty nice match.

She agreed. And wondered aloud that since he spent so much of his time at her place now—which was no surprise, given how roomy her condo was and how small and cramped his apartment—if it made sense for him to keep paying rent.

Virgel thought to say well, that was just the way of the world, but when he opened his mouth, he said "Right."

THE SHELL HOUSE

He couldn't take it all in, it was too much. Everywhere Pat McCandless looked were sea shells—in at least as many colors as were in his 48 crayon Crayola box: glazed pink, cobalt blue, magenta, apple green, coffee brown, butter yellow, salmon, lavender, apricot. And the shells came in all different patterns—zigzag, mottled, calico, spiral and zebra—and shapes—spiny, oval, boxy, cone, whorl and spire. The shell garden was like a life-size kaleidoscope.

Through a maze of encrusted walls with signs identifying the various shells in each section, Pat followed a narrow path of crushed shells. Each new turn held surprises—a bird bath of pinkish-violet fan shells, a row of bird houses covered with pale yellow tellins, a line of red shell ducklings. He passed through a low green arch into an open area holding a white pool filled with water. From the center of the pool rose a huge bird made of blue indigo shells, a crane with its wings spread wide and one foot touching down as it took off in flight. The crane's down leg looked a bit thick, but Pat knew how hard it was to get a sculpture to stand right. The "Mexican Clay Object" he'd made back in second grade looked more like a hippo than a deer, its slumped legs were so thick.

Nickels and pennies lay scattered on the pool bottom. He took a quarter—his allowance—and flipped it into the water. Ripples spread about the crane's foot as if it had moved.

Did the shell man make enough money to live off his garden and house? Didn't people steal coins when he wasn't looking? They stole them at St. Ann's. At the altar, snuffing candles after early mass Pat had seen a bum with a strip of wire trying to work coins up through the slot in the locked offering box. Pat told him to get away, but the bum paid him no attention. If one of the tough eighth grade altar boys had been there, he'd have booted the guy out.

Pat looked back along the path for Mom, but still didn't see her. Or Gil. He hadn't seen anyone else since he entered the maze. On a Saturday afternoon? When it cost only fifty cents? You'd think the place would be packed. Though it was October, a cool, gray day. Maybe in the summer a lot more people came.

A shell-encrusted bench faced the coin pool, and Pat stepped onto it to look back at the gate. Maybe Mom was out front talking to the artist, a stumpy old bald man in overalls who'd answered the bell pull. Gil Pratt, waving off her offer to pay, had given the man a couple of ones and told him to keep the change. But the artist counted out two quarters from a leather drawstring purse like a prospector's poke and handed them over along with a guide to "The Shell Garden." Would they remember please to leave the booklet when they left, he asked them. Some people didn't, though it was no good to them except when they were there. Taking it only made him have to print more. As he'd talked, he looked off to one side like it wasn't them he thought might make trouble, but some other people. His voice was so soft it made you worry what would happen to him if somebody came to rob him.

From his stance on the bench Pat could see the maze wasn't really a maze but just a walled walk with twists and turns, all of it shell-coated. Even the house itself, like a wizard's cottage, was covered in shells— roof, walls and porch, everything but the windows. Unless he'd seen it for himself, Pat wouldn't have believed it.

The mimeographed guide said the shells were trucked in from both coasts. That Pat could believe. But to think that one old man could cement tons of seashells in figures and patterns in his own backyard— that he dreamed up the shell garden in the first place— and that he had the nerve to cover his whole house with shells, that was unbelievable. In *Toledo?* Just around the corner from Champion Spark Plug? Where Mom had to work second trick Monday through Friday in grease and heat to make her quota of five thousand plugs a night? To find the shell house there was like walking down the front stairs from the apartment over Maloney's Bar & Grill and, instead of stepping onto Monroe Street, finding yourself in Paris, France.

He sat on the bench to wait for Mom to catch up.

The little booklet listed all the kinds of shells used: Limpet, zebra, periwinkle, star, helmet, conch, cowry, whelk, triton, nautilus, cone, mussel, cockle, screw, Venus. Who'd ever dream there were so many? And the names—Northern Horse, Lion's Paw, Shark's Eye, Turban, Lace, Tusk, Bleeding Tooth, Flamingo Tongue, Nipple, Virgin, Rock Eater, Sun and Moon ... *Jesus.*

Dad would like the shell house, Pat thought. When his hands weren't shaking, he liked to draw cartoons and show Pat how to do them. Kilroy Was Here—with a big nose hanging over a fence and two goggle eyes showing above it. When Dad got out of the Veteran's Hospital, maybe Pat could get him to come see the place. Dad and the artist would probably get along. In France after the Armistice Dad had walked guard duty by some murals, beautiful paintings that took up whole walls of buildings.

When it started spitting rain, Pat headed back.

At the gate he saw Mom sitting with Gil in his new '54 pearl gray Studebaker coupe with a dark cranberry top. She had her hair waved in front like Ida Lupino, her favorite actress. A green and yellow scarf wrapped about her neck, she was talking and jabbing the air with a cigarette. Gil nodded, his pink sports car cap bobbing. She turned away from him to her window, her jaw set hard. Seeing Pat, she rolled down the glass, flipped out her cigarette, and motioned for him to come.

He dropped the guide through the porch door slot and went to the car.

"Potsy, I thought you were never coming back." Mom swung open the door and leaned forward to tilt up her seat back.

"I stuck up for you," Gil said. "I said you had enough sense to come in out of the rain."

Pat jammed himself into the narrow rear seat under the coupe's low roof.

Gil glanced back at him. "Place is something else, huh?" He wore the collar of his puffy white nylon jacket turned up like the cool guys in high school. "Guy must've blown a bundle on those clamshells, huh?"

"Where were you?" Pat asked Mom.

"Oh, we looked around, the house and all."

"Not much, you didn't."

"I thought it was pretty," she said.

"You didn't see the pool in back."

"Well, I saw what I wanted."

"What, the porch?"

"Don't get smart." She turned to face him. "We came so *you* could see it. The least you could do is to thank Mr. Pratt."

Lighting a cigarette, Gil shook his head. "Gil," he said, exhaling. "And don't bug him about it, it was my treat." He started the Studebaker, clicked on the wipers, and drove down Victory, a narrow side street crowded by small neat houses sided with fake brick.

Gil flicked a look at Pat. "Me, I saw it already. Came with a friend of mine."

Mom cocked her head and Gil laughed. "Nah, nah. A *guy* I shoot pool with. He'd worked at the steel mill with that character, the shell man. Old Kraut always missing work, one thing or another wrong with him, Republic gave him the boot. A guy like that, how's he get by? Disability maybe. You look at the place, you know he's not playing with a full deck."

At Montrose he took a left.

Mom looked at Pat. "But you had fun?"

"I said."

"Oh?" She smiled as though to prompt him, then waited, the smile fading. Her forearm lay on the seat back, the fingers of her left hand bare. She never wore her wedding ring to work because she was afraid she'd lose it, she said, but now the only time she wore it was at Sunday mass. "Well, if you said it, I didn't hear you."

He looked out the little triangle of window beside him. "I said it back by the pool that you didn't see."

"I don't know what your problem is, but I know I've had enough of it," she said, turning her back on him.

Pat slouched down in the seat. The toe of his Keds bumped something. Leaning sideways he saw the sharp end of a jack handle beneath Gil's seat.

"Maddie, relax." Gil took the cigarette from his mouth and put it between her lips. "I was his age, I was a wise-ass too." He winked at Pat. "What's eating you, sport? Shell-shocked?"

Mom coughed smoke.

"Oops, right." Gil ducked his head. "Sorry. No offense to the mister. I know the war messed him up bad. But I meant seashells, you know, at the shell house. Just trying to make a joke, get a smile out of Buster Brown back there."

"Well, don't," Mom said. "It's not your job."

"Gotcha." He coasted through a stop at Dorr Street.

With the sole of his shoe Pat dragged the jack handle from under the seat.

"I can't solve everyone's problems," Mom said. "I'm only one person."

"Nobody's asking you to solve their problems," Gil told her. "He's a big boy now, he can handle himself. Right, buddy?"

Pat told Mom he was sorry if he'd sounded sarcastic.

"Oh," she said. "I know. It's not you, Potsy. I'm just tired."

"I know how to fix that," Gil said. "Go dancing, it'll pep you up."

Maybe when Dad was back from Brecksville Gil would wise up and let Mom alone. Though, dumb as he was, maybe he wouldn't.

Pat dropped his Mud Hens cap to the floor, bent to pick it up, and slid the jack handle up under his zipped windbreaker. When Dad got home he would give it to him as a present, saying he found it.

So Dad would have it handy when Gil came sneaking around.

WHERE THE DREAM BEGINS

Bud "Buster" Brophy hung the afternoon's damp hand wraps from a low overhead steam pipe and started gathering a scatter of sparring mitts. How many times did he have to tell these bums to pick up after themselves? That was the trouble with fighters, they never grew up. Even the over-the-hill ones still thought of themselves as contenders waiting for their big break.

Once again, he phoned Damon's mother to ask if she knew where he was, and once again, she swore she hadn't seen him. Bud thanked her kindly, although he knew damned well that she'd lie to his face to protect her mama's boy. Never had she wanted her boy to follow in his absentee father's footsteps. Bad enough that the man had been a drunken whoremonger, but she'd felt for sure that his ending up punch drunk in a state home wearing a diaper and babbling like a baby was enough to keep the boy a world away from boxing. But no, he had a stubborn streak like his father and was bound and determined to show he could do better as a heavyweight than light-heavy Billy "Night Night" Dyson had ever done.

The side door that was the Pound 4 Pound front door burst open. "I found him!"

"How many damn times I gotta tell you? Don't slam that—"

"No shit. I really did. Really!"

Bud eyed Cadge. The gaunt bum looked halfway sober, a rare state for him this late in the day. Meaning he really might have spotted the kid or was so desperate for a handout he'd risk a whipping to get it.

"No shit now?"

"God's honest truth."

"Where is he?"

"Santa Monica Beach."

"Okay, let's go."

"Where's my fiver?"

"Seeing is believing."

He spotted his boy right off. The stupid son of a bitch! What had Bud ever done to deserve such betrayal? He maneuvered his van into the right lane, parked in the lot, hopped out and, leaving Cadge in his wake, hobbled and slid as fast as he could down the grassy slope to the beach.

God Almighty, would you look at him now! Big as life, shadow-boxing for a gaggle of fans, signing autographs, having his picture taken. And, of all the gall, he had a posterboard propped on an easel: MEET THE NEXT HEAVYWEIGHT CHAMPION OF THE WORLD! DAMON "DYNAMITE" DYSON!

Bud elbowed people from his way to face his boy. "What in hell you think you're doing?"

"Autograph, picture, six bucks each, both for ten. Get in line, sir, please wait your turn."

Cadge, gasping, said, "I told you straight, right? Where's my fiver?"

Bud ignored him, eyes glued to his fighter. He held up his hands, palms open, truce. "Look, Damon ... Dynamite, I know I been riding you hard, but only for your own good. A fighter gets a shot at the title maybe once in his career, *if* he's lucky. This is your shot, son. Don't sell yourself short for chump change."

Dynamite eyed him nervously, looking like he might make a run for it.

"You back on drugs, that it? Okay, I'll get you to a doctor. We'll work things out."

His boy picked up the easel and placard.

"That's the ticket. We can ease up on road work and the sand bags. It's time to get more sparring in anyhow. Work on those triple hooks. You'll catch that street punk taking you for just another bum of the month, and you'll flatten his ass. You'll wear the championship belt with pride. A hero."

Dynamite nodded, but then suddenly sidestepped his manager/trainer and headed up the grassy slope. Bud stumbled after him, calling for Cadge to follow.

Halfway up the slope, heart hammering, he lunged, caught his boy by the ankle and brought him down. Dyson, strong as a bull, kept crawling up the slope dragging Brophy behind him. When they reached the top, Dynamite shook free of Bud, got to his feet, and stopped cold. Cadge blocked his way, his switchblade pointed at Dyson's heart.

Bud stood, hands on his knees, sucking air, his heart hammering like a speed bag. He was getting too old for this happy horseshit. When he'd gotten enough wind that it didn't seem he was about to pass out, he took a good look at his fighter. Who, he saw now, wasn't his fighter.

Up close you could tell the difference. The eyes, the ears. And the fake lacked the little love handles that the real Dynamite, no matter how hard he trained, never could get rid of completely.

"You bullshitter! I'll have you locked up for fraud. Identity theft. Embezzlement."

"No, man, don't send me away. Please!" Pulling out a wad of bills he offered it to Bud. "It's all there. Take it. I'int mean any trouble. Just trying to pay my room rent, man, okay?"

Bud waved off the cash, but Cadge flashed his blade. "Ten of that's mine." He snatched a ten spot from the wad. "Five for finding, five for stopping," he told Bud.

The hunk of muscle had tears in his eyes. "What you gone do to me?"

Bud stared at him for a moment. "How'd you like a job?"

"Follow with the right!"

Sparring partner Lucius "Thunder Fist" Smith, a slugger in the mode of Curtis "King" Conn, the current heavyweight champ, backed across the ring under the Dynamite look-alike's ragged but sustained assault. What the new boy lacked in technique and power, he made up for in action. His conditioning was great, even better than the real Dynamite's. He could windmill for a full minute without flagging, but Bud couldn't seem to get him to set down on his punches, quit slapping and turn them over, get some real power into them.

Not that the kid was anywhere near the fighter the real Dynamite was, but he didn't need to be. All he had to do was pass for Dynamite at tomorrow's media workout. If everything came off without a hitch, the reporters would get their news pics and TV clips and exit the gym none the wiser. The last thing in the world Bud needed was for the promoter to find out he had misplaced his fighter. If the match got bumped, Bud and Damon could lose out on the biggest payday of their careers. Two chumps, no champ.

And as lazy as the real Damon was, Bud knew he'd drag his ass back to the gym in time for his title shot. Training he hated; attention he loved.

When Damon finally did show, nine short days before their flight to Las Vegas, he looked like shit. Fat-assed, puffy-faced, soft! What a heart-breaking business boxing was. You wait your whole goddamned life for your moment in the spotlight and then some spoiled mama's boy ruins it for you. If Bud had to do it over again, he'd stay as far away from the sweet science as possible.

"What the hell you doing here?" Bud asked the sulking hulk.

"Come to fight, what you think?"

"*Now*? Look at you, pus-gut! You gotta be kidding. You'll be outta gas in two rounds."

"Won't go that far." He held up his meaty fists. 'Still got the punch. Only take one."

Bud gestured to the ring where Damon's substitute was belaboring a sparring partner with a barrage of punches. "I'm thinking maybe we oughtta go with him."

"Bullshit! Y'ain't putting no ringer in for me."

"Why not? We keep our mouth shut, pick up our check, you don't get killed."

Damon got to his feet. "Get me some gear, suit me up."

"Oh no, fat boy. I don't want your heart attack on my conscience."

"Bud, I know you got an excuse, being Caucasian and all, but I just don't know how you ever got to be old as you is being so *stupid*."

Damon was suited up and out of the locker room in five minutes, got another fighter to glove and headgear him when Bud refused to do it, climbed into the ring, told the sparring partner to beat it, shook hands with his double, waited for the round timer to sound, and flattened the fake Damon cold in 51 seconds.

Which, to give the devil his due, was a lot less than the two and two-thirds rounds that the real Damon lasted against Curtis "King" Conn in Las Vegas.

They avoided the press, picked up their money, and flew home. Bud tried to stay mad at Damon but couldn't do it. In a month's time they were in the gym, Bud pushing his boy hard, his boy responding beautifully. Maybe the kid had learned his lesson. Maybe he'd take training seriously now. They still were ranked in the heavyweight top ten, number eight; with a couple of good wins they could climb back within reach of a rematch. His boy would be the underdog, but America loved underdogs.

Bud had asked around about the fake Damon, who'd been carted off on a stretcher to the emergency ward the day of his K.O. and after two days in a coma had slipped out of the hospital without being released, and just disappeared. Cadge put out feelers, but nobody had seen him in his old haunts. Maybe he was holed up some place on a long drunk, or maybe he had brain damage and didn't remember who he was or where he lived and had just wandered off somewhere. Nobody knew anything.

Even nights when Bud lay awake asking himself who he thought he was kidding about Damon's comeback, come morning he got up and went to the gym to oversee his boy's treadmill and weight routines, work the punch mitts with him, take him through the basics, jab-jab-hook, jab-right cross, feint the jab, right to the body, left hook to the head, like a kid reciting the alphabet till he had it down cold. Hit and hurt, the language of boxing.

What else could you do? You couldn't just throw in the towel on one of your own.

AFTERWORD

"There are more tears shed over answered
prayers than over unanswered ones."
—Saint Teresa of Avila, 1515-1582

Whatever it was that Amanda shared with Paul, it
didn't last. What early in their marriage she had taken
for confidence she later recognized as arrogance. Yes,
he could cook and knew of comfy little bed and breakfast
hideaways for weekends away, was sexually skilled and
solicitous, but in time all of Paul's talk came to seem
squid's ink, camouflage for a spineless creature. Was
she being too harsh, unfair? If so, she no longer cared.

Not that she hadn't given it a try. At first, growing
tired of Paul, she had tried to feign interest but discovered
that she had no skill at dissembling. In her mind
hypocrisy ranked as a cardinal sin. It condemned people
to a nether world of false emotion, barely distinguishable
from scripted characters in a soap opera.

The unmistakable decline of her interest in Paul
led to one of his in her. While he seemed quite capable
of continuing in such a feigned relationship, she was
not. In the aftermath of their divorce, she packed up
her personal belongings and books, and moved into a
furnished one bedroom apartment on the third floor of
a restored Victorian on the edge of downtown. Having
escaped the roomy vacuity of the ostentatious suburban
split-level in the far suburbs where Paul chose to
remain, she prized her snug new quarters as a refuge.
Even if, on some rainy or snowy days, one could feel a
bit cloistered there.

Paul offered to let her take their four-year-old
compact (so he'd have an excuse to get the SUV he'd
had his eye on?) but she declined. The local bus service
covered the county and she had no extended travel plans.

The only books she read now were ones she'd read before, written by authors who deserved rereading: Austen, the Brontes, Dickens, James, Hardy. Knowing the ending from the beginning gave her a sense of security. Boredom she didn't mind; what caused pain was hope. More accurately, she thought, the pursuit of hope.

Her twenty-hour-a-week job as cashier at the nearby Book Nook allowed her to chat with people of similar interests, and the small paycheck supplemented her income from the money left to her in her mother's modest estate.

At the urging of her three-miles-three-days-a-week walking partner, Esther, she consulted a therapist. Two, actually: first a woman, next a man. Both suggested that her father's abandonment of the family when she was twelve and her mother's subsequent obsession with buying unneeded items at yard sales to bring home to an already over-packed house had left Amanda with abandonment issues. And, while both counselors seemed decent, well-intentioned people, their advice boiled down to the assumption that at heart a human being desired to be happy in life: not just calm, content, occupied or useful, but *happy*. After a time she stopped scheduling sessions.

Another friend, Mona, the district librarian, and she lunched together at least every other week. Amanda also was friendly with people on the Friends of the Library business committee and her fellow supporters of the County Arts museum, each of which met monthly.

From time to time she had attended services at the Episcopalian church, which she admired for its many good works in the community. The church's pastor, a ruddily handsome man who wore expensive suits, took to calling on her at home to counsel her through what he knew must be a difficult time in her life. She appreciated his concern, but at times felt she heard in his sonorous voice a tone that seemed less consoling than seductive. While she realized that it could be only her imagination, she backed away from his offered embraces and in time asked him not to drop by any longer.

Then the following summer she was surprised by her interest in another Paul—Paul II as she came to think of him—whom she had met at the county art museum's Friday wine and cheese gathering. Not that she was surprised to meet someone there as the gatherings were known to attract cultured singles.

Paul II's consuming interest was Florence in the Early Renaissance, and his interest in art history seemed a world away from Paul I's in money and social status. They hiked together in a nearby metropolitan park and, in autumn, spent a night together in a faux Swiss Chalet at a state park during which she discovered that he was as bland in bed as he was in conversing about anything but his specialty.

For a time they took up wine as an interest, ferreting out various vintages and labels in cozy little wine cellars as though they were trophies, and attending wine tasting seminars to learn of distinctions in clarity, integration, expressiveness, complexity, connectedness and color, the latter being judged best against a white background. And, while she dutifully spat her multiple sips into the brass spittoons provided—as tasters were advised to do to avoid intoxication—she felt embarrassed by the entire undertaking and stopped attending.

In the end Paul II proved as compatible in bed as he was at the dinner table, but at bottom he was supercilious and they arranged an amicable and alimony-free divorce.

Celibacy seemed to be her natural state. She wondered for a time if she had missed her calling as a Roman Catholic nun, but upon reflection realized that no, she could find no value in donning a black habit, incessantly repeating the same rote prayers, neither in Latin—which she preferred for the music of the language and its capacity to suspend thought— nor in English—which lacked Latin's enchantment and laid bare the childishness of the verse. Nor was she one to vow obedience to mother church.

Not that she was unhappy. What at one time she had feared most in her life, loneliness, she had discovered was something altogether different and sweeter: solitude.

Rehearsal

Early for rehearsal and not wanting to stand around outside the locked school and maybe get spotted and knocked around by Alvetas, Pat McCandless slipped into St. Ann's church. At the side altar to Saint Joseph he dropped a dime into the offering box before a rack of vigil lights and, with a wax taper, lighted a squat white candle in a red glass cup in thanks for having made it home safely from his hide out. Having eaten supper, washed up and put on clean clothes, he felt a bit better now. Not that he'd really been beaten up. His fight with Terry Irby was only a fake. Which was Irby's idea, a way for them to get out of having to fight each other for real after school in front of all the eighth grade guys. Because, after their run-in on the playground at recess, everybody knew Irby and McCandless would have to settle it later. Unless they wanted to be called chicken and maybe get beat up by the tough guys for weaseling out.

So on the way home for lunch they'd ducked into an empty garage and acted out a fight like in the movies, throwing themselves around, yelling and falling, then telling it over and over to each other to get their stories straight. Not wanting to tear his clothes like Irby, Pat had hit himself in the head with a brick hard enough to make a pretty good cut. That was what convinced the guys back at school that the fight was for real. So it seemed only right, especially since Irby didn't seem to care, that McCandless should say he won.

Pat touched the pad of white gauze taped above his left eye.

How the hell was he to know that Alvetas Coutsavakis, the third toughest guy in eighth grade, would claim winners?

Only one candle burned before Joseph, while across the church Mary's altar was lit up like a carnival.

Irby always went to Mary, saying why waste your prayers on a heavenly step-father. But Pat figured you had a better chance of being heard by someone who didn't draw such heavy traffic. He dug into his pockets and came up empty but fired up two candles anyway, one for the intention that Mom would keep making her quota of 5,000 plugs a night at Champion Spark Plug and one for Dad to get himself straightened out at the Veterans Hospital. Tomorrow he'd put what he owed in the box and kick in a dime as interest.

He knelt at the rail to pray for his intentions, especially that he not get his ass kicked by the Greek. Coutsavakis would have caught him after school if Pat hadn't ducked out the back way and, instead of going home, run down Monroe Street to the Toledo Art Museum to hide out where Pat's older sister Ann spent a lot of her time but no one would ever think of looking for *him*. Glory be to the Father, and to the Son. Finished praying, he crossed himself and stood.

Going down the aisle he took a pew that gave him a clear view of the side exits and knelt with a pillar at his back hiding him from anyone who came in the main doors. Without his glasses he saw the lighted vigil lights as fuzzy red globes, like roses. He wished the school nurse would have listened to him—he sat up front and saw fine, really. Now that his vision had been corrected, he found that seeing things clearly was a real disappointment. Before, he'd never noticed all the chipped bricks and pigeon shit out front of their apartment or the wrinkles at the corners of Mom's eyes. The first time he had worn his glasses to church he was shocked to see that the lights outlining the nave were bare light bulbs, though what he'd thought they were, he had no idea. But blurred, they had looked like stars, pulsing as he squinted. Now, even when he took off the glasses, he knew they were just plain white bulbs like Mom bought at Lickendorf's Hardware.

A squeak sounded from the rear, like one of the main doors opening. He turned, hunching behind the pillar, and waited for someone to show himself. And waited, seeing no one. But he was sure he'd heard a door open. Why would anyone sneak into church unless they were after someone? Slowly and quietly he slid from his seat to his hands and knees and crawled from the pew. If he made a break for it, the Greek and his gang would run him down easy. He crept up the side aisle, keeping close to the pews. On the wall above him were pictured the stations on the way of the cross where Jesus spoke to the women, Jesus was stripped of His garments; Jesus fell for the third time. He eased open the half-door to the center stall of the confessional and crawled inside, the soft thick purple curtains dragging over his back. In the close dark he sat on the priest's seat and steadied his breathing. With a finger he split the curtain a tiny bit, but saw no one. Alvetas had looked around and left? Or was he waiting for Pat to panic? Or was the church empty and it was just Pat's imagination? Not about to find out, he slowly closed the curtain.

As his eyes adjusted to the dark, he saw that the priest's place wasn't all that different from the sinners', except that the seat was padded and not bare wood. Even so, it had to be hard to sit there hour after hour while people unloaded their sins on you. Every Saturday Pat came in with a ton of sins to confess and now had started showing up for Wednesday evening confessions too. It was either that or stop taking communion mornings. He had to learn to keep his hands off himself. If he didn't, pretty soon he'd have to make confession every day of the week, sneaking into other parishes to hide what a sinner he was from Fathers Hauff and Urbanski. *Man, oh man.* Yet he liked confession, really, even more than communion. Nothing made you feel better faster than a good confession. You went in feeling dirty as a rat, trapped, hopeless, and came out absolved of your sins and, once you'd said your penance, *free.* When you left church and stood on the front steps, breathing deep, everything felt new. Even the air smelled fresher, clean and waxy, like new modeling clay. Given another chance, you swore to keep your soul, the temple of the Holy Spirit, pure for as long as you lived or as long as possible anyway. At least for the rest of the week, you hoped.

Leaning back on the padded seat, Pat stretched out his legs. It had to feel pretty good being a priest and having the power to forgive. Though maybe it got under your skin getting the same people week after week with the same sins, no matter how big a penance you'd laid on them last time. Still, it'd be neat to know who in the parish was doing what. What did Victoria Starrett confess, he wondered, as she knelt at the little grated window in the dark, telling her secrets? Jeez, what if that was *her* Pat heard come in. What if she came to confession now? Maybe she'd stopped by church to pray that she wouldn't screw up at play rehearsal but then noticed somehow that someone was in the confessional booth—in the priest's place, so who could it be but a priest? She'd come in and kneel and whisper in Pat's ear, "Bless me, father, for I have sinned," telling him what she let Jim King do on the dates they weren't allowed to have yet, the nights she told her folks she was going to the movies with girlfriends, but put on red lipstick and a pink sweater to meet King at the Avalon and sit in the balcony and make out.

Oh Jeez! Whenever he thought about her, he got hard, he couldn't help it, it just happened. But in the *confessional?* He shoved his stiff thing down and away like it was a lever to turn off a machine. Crossing his arms on his chest, he clamped his hands in his armpits. His dingus strained against his corduroys like Dracula pushing at the lid of his coffin. *Jesus, Mary, and Joseph, pray for us now and at the hour of our death. Saint Maria Goretti, give us pure thoughts and keep us from ...* But how the hell could you help but think about it, that's all some guys ever talked about. Like that creep Dickie Kleinschmidt, always twisting things. "Remember what Sister told you, boys, don't forget your ejaculations!"

Hearing a noise, he sat perfectly still, holding his breath. It wasn't his imagination. Someone else was there with him. Slowly, he took a peek. Across the church stood the ancient Italian who groaned and nodded in a front pew every morning at the 6:30 side altar mass that Pat served for Father Hauff. The old man leaned on the rail in front of the Virgin Mother's altar. The candlelight made his sunken face look like a skull. He looked around him, then lifted his cane and used its tip to snuff out all the vigil lights.

        *   *   *

"Ah! The early bird!" Hazel said as Pat turned the corner from church to school. "I've only just arrived myself." He held up a ring of keys, jangling them like bells. Harold Hazelton was his real name but the kids all called him Hazel, though not to his face. He cocked his head, looking at the bandage. "And what's this?"

"A cut. I was in a fight."

"Oh. I'm sorry to hear that."

"It's okay. I won."

"But you're badly hurt?"

"No, I'm okay."

"Then do you really need something that large?"

Pat shrugged his shoulders. The cut wasn't that big, more of a scrape really, but the bandage made sure people noticed.

"Well, I'm certain it will be off by opening night."

Inside, Hazel hooked open the outer door and flipped on the hall light. Pat followed him through swinging doors into the auditorium with its linoleum block floor and the small raised stage where Petronilla stood to make announcements at assembly.

"I'll look to the lights. Perhaps you'd set up chairs?"

"Sure." He dragged folding wooden chairs from a stack at the back of the room and kicked them open. Kids made fun of Hazel because of his purple beret and peach fuzz mustache and his being a grown man without a real job who still lived at home with his mother, but Pat didn't mind him. Hazel helped out with the choir and the altar society and now with the drama club too. People said he had missed his calling and should have been a priest but some guys said no he couldn't because he was a queer.

Mrs. Hazelton, Harold's mother, the church organist, was a widow who wore black dresses and a wide brimmed black hat with a purple peacock feather. She was the fattest person Pat ever had seen outside the circus. It was something to see her climb the narrow, winding stairs to the organ loft, especially if you were right behind her. Her hips in the black dress rubbed the white walls like giant erasers and she had to stop and rest every other step to catch her breath.

There was no way you could get around her; you just had to wait until she moved again. If she got any fatter she'd get stuck in the stairway and they'd have to starve her out or knock down a wall. Oh how the poor soul suffered, the old women of the parish said, and what a saint she was to make such lovely music for them all. But in choir when you saw her play, when she pulled out the stops and would close her eyes and throw back her head, her face wet with sweat and her triple chin trembling with the power of the giant pipes, you knew that the organ was her big thrill.

Auditorium lights on, Hazel came down from the stage. "Oh stop, stop, that was more than enough chairs, thank you. There'll be no audience tonight. ... No, leave them be. I can put them back later."

Pat sat on one of the unfolded chairs.

"Here you are," Hazel said, "a pencil for notes. Aaaaand—" He handed over a small orange book, *A Minor Miracle*. Only a one-act, yes, but they should consider themselves lucky to have the chance to do anything at all in the parish, given the circumstances. Pastor Hauff had been so obdurate over the years, but now, thanks to young Father Urbanski, they had the good fortune to be part of St. Ann's premiere production.

On the cover of Pat's script someone had written "Father" in pencil. At try-outs, where they had only blurred mimeographed sheets of character descriptions and part of a scene because Hazel didn't want the scripts walking off, Pat had wanted to read for Larry, the boyfriend. He knew the part of the girlfriend was a shoo-in for Victoria. But Hazel had him read for the father. A challenging role, he'd said, demanding intelligence and maturity. Though Pat knew Hazel pegged him for it because he was fat and wore glasses and looked old, like Dotty Skalski, cast as the mother.

"That's yours to keep until we're off book," Hazel said. "And from this moment on I want you to think of yourself as Mr. Charles Brightwell, to go to sleep nights and wake up mornings in character. You'll be called Patrick McCandless at school of course and must answer to that, but you'll know that truly, at least for the time being, you are someone else, Mr. Charles Brightwell. That's the ideal anyway, the way a fine actor becomes the role rather than merely indicating it." Hazel looked at the tiny stage with its frayed green curtain. "Well. We'll just have to do the best we can with what we have. And try not to embarrass ourselves."

Though Pat had never read a play, he'd expected it to be a book. But the script was as thin as the stapled song pamphlets passed out in music class and its orange cover no thicker than the construction paper used to cut pumpkins from for Halloween decorations. His copy was dog-eared and creased and, inside, the father's speeches were underlined in pencil and scribbled in the narrow margins were notes: Stand Up, Walk Around, Get Mad. He guessed, too, that he had expected their group to be the first to do the play. Now he wondered who else had been Mr. Charles Brightwell, a stern but fair man, vest buttoned, tie loosened, and how good he'd been at it.

He began erasing the penciled notes so he wouldn't feel like he was only copying someone else's way of doing things, but the paper tore so easily that he stopped. You could see right through the pages and the print was so tiny you about had to touch it with your nose to read it.

The living room of the Brightwell home, comfortable but not showy. On the fireplace mantle stands a statue of St. Jude, Patron Saint of the Hopeless. On the table beside the armchair are a pipe and a tobacco pouch.

It sounded like directions to a model airplane kit. It was nothing like *The Call of the Wild* or *Boru, The Story of an Irish Wolfhound* which Pat took out of the library over and over again. Reading those, he got completely lost in the story, feeling the fear of the dog being beaten and the rush of excitement when its wolf part came out and turned on its enemies and tore them apart. *A Minor Miracle*, though, with the characters' names in capitals like headings in an outline, stayed just words on a page.

MR. BRIGHTWELL: (*lighting his pipe*) Really now, don't you think it best—

KATHLEEN: (*peering out the window*) No!
Oh, I don't know!

He only hoped that once he had his part memorized he could forget about the script and act the father well enough to make people believe in him.

Dotty Skalski showed up right on time and plunked herself down beside him, her moon face covered with freckles like the measles. Gee, she was excited to get in the play, wasn't he? Weren't they lucky ducks though!

Pat said he had to study his role and she left to chat with Hazel.

He hoped Victoria would show up alone, but when she finally came, twenty minutes late, she was with King. Hazel lectured the cast then on the importance of punctuality. They had only four weeks until the night of the performance, sixteen rehearsals in all, and they would need every precious minute. He arranged their chairs in a half-circle, Pat and Dotty to one side of him, Jim and Victoria to the other. Pat watched Victoria scooch her chair closer to King's and dangle a hand to touch his. Man, he just didn't get it. Jim King bossed her around and called her "Vick," when not in a million years was she a Vick. She had to be blind not to see what a jerk he was. Which was her only fault that Pat could see, but a serious one as far his chances with her went. Last week at benediction, after choir, Caroline Longeway had told him that Jim and Vicky had traded rings, which really shook up Pat. Going steady would mean serious trouble for them if the nuns found out, but he couldn't think of a way to spill the beans on King without getting Victoria in Dutch too.

Before they launched into the read-through, Hazel said, he wished to stress that during all rehearsals he would address them and wanted them to address one another by their character names only. The moment they stepped into that auditorium they became Larry and Kathleen, Mr. and Mrs. Brightwell. The kids all gave each other sidelong looks, but nobody said anything, and Hazel began reading the stage directions.

In the middle of Pat's first speech, Hazel held up a hand to stop him. "Mr. Brightwell? Shouldn't you be wearing glasses?"

Mr. Brightwell didn't wear glasses.

Hazel smiled. "Oh, but I think he does."

Not according to the script he didn't.

"Yes, well, very good, but wear them from now on please. We can't see your face with it buried in the script."

"When I learn my lines, I won't need a script."

"In the meantime. Continue, please."

Every so often during the reading Hazel called a halt to tell them how to sound and what they were feeling. "Kathleen, imagine how frustrated you are right now." It was odd hearing Victoria called Kathleen. It confused her at first but she got used to it. Yet about every time Hazel called on Larry, Jim would ask. "Who?" "There an owl in here?" Pat said into his script. He and Dotty had no trouble answering to Mr. and Mrs. Brightwell, but then they were happy to be other people for a change. King and Starrett didn't want to be anyone else but themselves.

Being called by another name made you feel a bit like you did when the nuns called the roll, always saying your last name first: Granata, John; Kretowicz, Emil; McCandless, Patrick. It felt funny to hear your name that way, as though you were your family before you were yourself. When the nun wasn't looking, the boys would roll their eyes and shake their heads at yet another dumb thing they had to put up with in school. And back in the lower grades, he remembered, no matter how many times they'd heard it they always would sniff and snort when King, James was called, like it was a joke the dim sister didn't get. On the playground they teased him about it, "Oh King James! Your hine-ass!" But as it turned out, Jim King *was* a highness compared to them. Girls loved his brown eyes and wavy blond hair, and guys wished they could throw a football like he could. He was the best quarterback St. Ann's had ever had.

But not a good reader. Victoria had to keep prompting him and then Hazel would walk him through the speech. "No, there's a period, see? So you stop there. And try not to say everything in the same tone of voice." Pat groaned as King stumbled over another passage but Hazel frowned at him, saying that one couldn't expect things to sail along right from the start. When finally they made it through the whole one-act, he told them to get on stage and try it again. Victoria sighed and he caught it. "As you should recall, I warned you all at auditions that I'd be working you hard. And you all assured me you were willing to give it your best, like real actors. All right?" He clapped his hands. "On stage!"

They read standing in a row like fence posts until he told them to feel free to move about as the moment might call for. Pat's feet hurt from standing still so he started walking around when he had lines, waving an arm or clenching a fist. After a while Dotty moved too, but not King or Starrett. It was like they were nailed in place. Victoria couldn't act but she was a pretty girl playing a pretty girl and Pat thought she'd do okay. But King, the talking brick, should never have been cast. Unless Hazel figured that with two of the most popular kids in school in the play more people would come see it.

It felt weird to Pat hearing Victoria call him "Father." In a way it made her seem close to him yet in another way farther away than ever. Then, too, it just sounded funny. Pat didn't know anyone who called their father "Father" and mother "Mother." He called his dad "Dad," although Ann sometimes called him "Daddy," and in school nearly everyone else said "Dad," except Kretowicz and Coci and Dotty Skalski who said "Papa" and Vern Rivere "Pop" and Kleinschmidt "the old man." In the script, though, it was all Father this, Father that, and Oh Mother, do you think we might... But it was just a play. And not a very good one either, Pat thought. Larry Worthington, a Catholic teenager, wanted Kathleen Brightwell, another Catholic teenager, to sneak out with him to an un-chaperoned dance. She'd agreed to but felt so bad about it that at home she kept losing her temper or breaking into tears over the least little thing. Mr. Brightwell wanted to call a doctor and Mrs. Brightwell thought their daughter should see a priest, but then in a temper tantrum Kathleen threw the statue of St. Jude out the window and accidentally hit Larry who was hanging around outside. He let out a yell and got dragged bleeding into the house by Kathleen's father, had his head bandaged by Kathleen's mother, and ended up confessing his plan and apologizing. Other than the statue scene, it was pretty boring really. The seventh and eighth graders, the kids who the play was for, would know right away that Kathleen wasn't going to sneak off anywhere with Larry. Because if she did, they wouldn't be seeing the play, not at St. Ann's. And, though Pat liked getting a chance as the father to tell somebody off, his speeches were just more of the same stuff they'd got from the nuns for eight years now: don't ask questions, obey the rules, don't cause trouble.

But Hurricane Hazel! He acted like the play was "The Greatest Show on Earth" and his cast were Charlton Heston, Betty Hutton, Cornel Wilde and Dorothy Lamour, instead of Jim, Victoria, Pat and Dotty. Perched on the lip of the stage, scribbling in his script, he'd call out "Anger, anger, show some fire!" or "You're sad, dear, let your shoulders slump." He got so worked up you felt embarrassed for him.

Although, really, it was more than just Hazel. There was something embarrassing about watching kids you'd known since first grade pretend to be someone else and feel certain things when you knew who they really were and that the feelings were faked. Which meant the others must have been really embarrassed by Pat, who was coming on strong as the head of the family. But hamming it up made it easier for him. The more he exaggerated his part, the less it seemed to have to do with him, so that it felt like he was standing off to one side watching someone else in his place pretending to be happy or sad. What he actually felt, though he tried not to show it so Victoria wouldn't think he was a jerk, was excited. Because even if the play was for morons he was happy to be in it. He liked how playing a role let you feel you could be anyone you wanted to be if you just acted that way and didn't let anyone see who you really were.

Then the weirdest thing happened. Pat was standing back out of the way as Mrs. Brightwell went through the motions of bandaging Larry Worthington's head when a strange feeling came over him. Not a feeling exactly but more of a picture in his mind—like a vision except that it wasn't religious, though what he saw was the photograph of his First Communion class. Forty-five first graders stood in rows on rising steps, all in white dresses and white suits, Pat one of only two boys in short pants, a pair just like new that Mom had found at the Goodwill store, and the only one in the whole class wearing saddle shoes which Dad had said were still the rage. The first graders held prayer books and rosaries in their clasped hands, the boys' books black, the girls' white, and the girls all wore white veils like little brides. One boy, Riordan, had a big monkey grin on his face but the rest of the class looked serious and saintly, even Mangan, as if they were being sent to do battle for Jesus. And all of them, Dotty, Jim, Victoria, were just little kids, still pudgy, their soft faces sort of blank, like lumps of clay. To see them back then, five rows of angels in white, you'd never have guessed that by eighth grade Alvetas would turn out to be a bully, Mayes a sneak, Kleinschmidt a creep, and poor Dotty Skalski such a skag. Or that Victoria Starrett, just another lump in first grade, would be so beautiful that every guy at St. Ann's wished she were his girl, and Jim King would be like a god to the rest of the class, and Pat would still be pretty much a lump.

At the play's end Mr. Brightwell got the final lines. He told Larry not to show his face at the house again until he had gone to confession and said a novena to St. Jude to thank him for knocking some sense into his head. "Hold for a laugh there," Hazel called. Mr. Brightwell laid a hand on Larry's shoulder. "I hope," he said, "this will be a lesson to you, son," then gave him a sharp shove that came as a surprise to everyone, even Pat, and sent King stumbling backwards.

"Hey! Watch it, dork!"

Hazel asked Mr. Brightwell just what he thought he was doing.

"I want him to leave now, don't I?"

Frowning, King faced Pat, who acted as if nothing had happened.

"Well," Hazel said. "Yes, that business might fit. Let's keep it for now, see how it wears."

Jim said "What, he gets to push me around?"

"Mr. Brightwell wants Larry to leave, doesn't he?"

"So you mean it's okay?"

"Yesss," Hazel said, dragging the s to show his strained patience. "All right. Again, please."

This time when Pat shoved King it was like trying to move a horse.

"Larry," Hazel said. And when Jim didn't look up— "James. Don't stiffen so. Don't anticipate. Allow yourself to be surprised. That's the whole secret of theater— discovery! Once more, please."

"I hope this will be a lesson to you, son." Pat felt the hard chest fall away from his touch. Then Mr. Brightwell turned, holding out a hand to his daughter. To his amazement, Victoria, as though controlled by some secret magnetic power stepped to his side and took his hand. Pat felt the blood rush to his face. "Let this be a lesson to us all."

"And curtain!" Hazel cried.

RINGOLEVIO

Driving back, Bonnie at the wheel, she told Bill how he had let her down yet again. In fact, she was beginning to wonder why in hell she even put up with him.

In the back seat of her bug, the caged cats yowled. As they had since Bill packed the car in Colorado—*mowr mowr*—and kept it up across Kansas and now into Missouri, the Show-Me state.

Bonnie was still pissed about leaving the mountains.

"It's just *so* fucking beautiful there!"

"I know, I know."

"Yet we're headed back to Ohio? I mean, *damn!*"

Bill himself felt more at home in flat land, but knew better than to say so. It was a long, slow trip home, what with her VW's engine missing on one cylinder, but he wasn't about to complain of the bug's shitty condition. Else Bonnie would start in on how she had wanted them to take his Harley. Remember?

Why can't we take your hog?

Not safe enough in the mountains.

But it'd be so wild!

Nope.

You don't want my legs wrapped around you?

It won't handle us and all our stuff.

All the way out and back, rumbling and vibrating? Think how many times you'd make me come.

Nope means nope.

Bonnie sighed. "I just know we could be happy living in the mountains."

"Long as I got you, I can't be any happier."

"Oh, you sweet-talking stud, you."

He squeezed her thigh, firm and hot. Strong. In bed with you on top and those long smooth legs locked onto you and the two of you coming down the home stretch neck and neck and then, *Jesus Christ Almighty,* hitting the finish line together? Man, oh man! Like dying and rising to Heaven.

He tugged at his jeans, working his throb rod to one side where it didn't have to fight the zipper. "But you know," he said, "Ohio's our home and all."

"Just because you're born in a place doesn't mean you have to stay there."

"And in the fall the leaves are really pretty."

"Prettier than aspens?"

"I'm just saying that that's *something* good Ohio's got."

"Poor baby," Bonnie said, patting him on the cheek, like she'd done in Colorado when he had complained about them staying there so long. Treating him like a moron in front of those shaggy beatnik fuckers. "Oh, poor Billy. I had no idea how abused you felt. Maybe you ought to go someplace you like better. Ride the thumb back to Ohio, why don't you?" Because she knew how much he *loved* the Buckeye state. So flat and boring, so peaceful. Such a great place to do nothing but work and sleep and feel sorry for yourself—all of Bill's favorite pastimes.

Sometimes he just *ached* to tee off on her! But it would be a cowardly thing to do, hit a woman, and a thing he had never yet done in his lifetime.

"Hey," he'd said. "Come on, Bonnie."

No! Go if he wanted to. She was happy right where she was.

Maybe he should take off, he had told her to her face. See how *she* liked getting dumped for a change. Bonnie only smiled at him. She knew he'd never do that and she was right; he hadn't. Bonnie was no one to be lonely for long. Not with Colorado guys buzzing 'round her like she was the queen bee. They sensed what Bill knew for a fact. Like no one else, at least no woman he had ever known, not even some pretty expensive whores, Bonnie Jo Pike could drive you out of your fucking mind. It was like ... like she was just all holes needing to be filled. She wanted it everywhere and all the time. Bill tried his damnedest to keep her happy, or at least to keep her from complaining, but nothing he did was ever enough. Which sometimes scared him even more than excited him. Like she was a she-devil like the one he'd seen in a late night horror movie on TV, a beautiful but evil witch sent to earth to punish men for being men by driving them nuts. Most every man Bonnie met wanted to be the one to satisfy her, but none of them could. Like in the movie she ate their hearts out and left them hollow as zombies to wander about in graveyards.

One of her old boyfriends, a married guy, wanted her to himself so bad that he tried to strangle her, she told Bill, but couldn't go through with it. Same problem he had in bed, Bonnie said. How she pitied his wife.

But someday, Bill thought, somebody might actually kill her. That's what scared him. What would he do without her?

It wasn't like he wanted to leave her, he told her. No way. He just worried that their money would run out and they'd end up stranded there.

"You can't be stranded in a place you want to be, dummy." And besides, Bonnie reminded him, they had sublet their apartment in Ohio for forty bucks a month more than their rent, remember? A clear profit—in cash. Okay?

No, it wasn't okay, he had told her, liking the look of surprise on her face. Way Bill figured it, the sublet money would maybe pay for about half the gas they burned getting to and from Colorado plus all the driving back and forth to work five days a week. Commuting, he said. That was all they were doing there. Is that what she wanted them to be now? Fucking commuters!

A wise-ass crack that, despite his many apologies, got him booted out of the sack, leaving him curled on the braid rug beside the big brass canopied bed; that being the closest Bonnie would let him get to her. The cats, Mick and Cher, looked down at him like hey, what're you doing down there? Not joining him though, oh no, they'd rather sleep with Bonnie. Who wouldn't?

Still, it seemed unfair. Bill was the one took care of the cats most of the time. Bonnie liked them okay, but didn't seem to really love them. Bill, he loved all animals. Pretty near all anyways. Though the summer he was nine when his mom went to California to see if maybe they could do better out there and her dead brother's wife, Aunt Helen, let him stay with her on her farm up in Michigan, he was scared of almost all the animals. The cows were huge and had horns, the rooster with its big scaly claws flew at your face for no reason and the chickens pecked your hands when you went to the coop to gather eggs like your aunt told you to do. But the big mongrel dogs, Alec and Nicky, and the old stinky Irish setter Clancy, treated Bill like a brother. He would sneak downstairs nights while his aunt snored and crawl behind the kitchen's big potbellied stove where the smelly dogs slept on a ratty old rug and curl up with them. They licked his face and hands and cuddled up to him and made him feel safe.

On the rug beside Bonnie's bed, the nights were long and lonely, and when he couldn't sleep he'd slip from his wallet a folded square of toilet paper he had scavenged from the wastebasket in the bathroom where Bonnie blotted her lipstick. In the glow of a penlight he stared at the imprint of her lips, that round red open mouth that could drive you nuts, especially when she said how starved she was for meat. It made him hard as a ball bat remembering how they had been starting out on their big trip west, giddy as kids, horny as goats, bouncing motel beds like trampolines. He could shut his eyes any time and see it over and over again like a favorite movie: *The Wonderful Honeymoon* starring Bonnie Jo Pike and Bill Dunlop, Jr. Though really they weren't married. And never would be, he knew. Like Bonnie told him and her other guys, nobody owned Bonnie Jo Pike and nobody ever would.

Finally, one night Bonnie had looked over the edge of the bed, praised Bill for being such a good guard dog and said, "All right already, quit beating your meat and come up and get some."

Talk about being happy!

But now things had gone bad again. Last night at a Super 8 just over the Indiana state line, Bonnie had said no to them sharing a room, not even a twin bed one, and got herself a single.

Bill, pretty near broke, said he guessed he'd have to sleep in the car then.

Bonnie nodded.

She'd take the cats with her, right?

She shook her head. Her room was no pets. But he could get a pets-allowed one or leave them in the car and get himself a single.

Nope. Too low on cash.

Well then, Mick and Cher and he could cozy up in the car. Wasn't he the lucky man? Getting to sleep with two pussies at once.

So he'd spent the night in the bug's front passenger seat, a cramped space but a bit roomier without the steering wheel. He dozed off and on but got little real sleep what with Mick and Cher meowing even though he'd fed them and taken the out on their leashes twice to pee and poop.

Behind the wheel, Bill tipped the stiff brim of his black Stetson forward to shade his eyes. It made him look like some city dude playing he was Rowdy Yates on *Rawhide*, Bill's favorite show, Clint Eastwood next to John Wayne being his favorite actor. But Bonnie had bought him the Stetson and liked him to wear it for her. Especially in bed, so he did.

Day one in Colorado Bonnie had started saying how they ought to move there, her smile and eyes lighting up as she did so. It could be a fresh start for both of them. A bullshit idea, Bill thought, but he kept his mouth shut. At least she said they should move there, not just her. And, knowing Bonnie, you knew she couldn't help but fall hard for the little settlement of Ward. Free love, hand-rolled joints passed around, skinny hippies and vegetarians living in a string of failed tourist cabins, in big old paint-flaked houses or flat-tired campers and engine-gutted trucks and vans; tribal gatherings around a rock-ringed fire pit at night, guitars and folk songs, everyone all wild hair and weird beards, some sitting in yoga positions, others sprawled on the ground like the bindle stiffs and boozers by the railroad tracks in Youngstown when Bill was a boy.

But it seemed to make Bonnie happy, so Bill kept his trap shut.

The guru in Ward was some lippy hippie dickwad called himself *True Man*, spelling it out for you so you wouldn't think it was *Truman* like that racist, genocidal war-mongering, Atomic-Bomb-dropping presidential asshole moral fucking coward Harry S. Bill thinking, right, because True Man was a different kind of asshole. The kind when you asked him how many miles roundtrip to Boulder he told you 11.26 klicks, like he'd been to 'Nam, man, though you knew sure as shit he'd hadn't. True Man wasn't about to risk losing his balls to a land mine, no fucking way. True Man was smart. Either he had flunked the Army's basic I.Q. test on purpose or found God and declared himself a pacifist.

Bill asked him right out was he a C.O. and True fucking Man said of course he was, as anyone with any moral sense should be. Unless they wanted to be like Lieutenant Calley and massacre unarmed civilians—women and children—like at My Lai. Was he Bill's hero? Calley?

No way, Bill told him, My Lai was an awful thing, terrible. It never should've happened. Bill was glad he hadn't been a soldier there.

"So you *can* think," True Man said, "good for you."

Bill let it slide. Thinking how much he had wanted to be a soldier and be sent off to fight a war. Then come home with medals on his chest and march down Main Street with other soldiers in a big parade: bands playing, flags flying, old men saluting you, young girls blowing you kisses, everyone clapping for their American heroes. It wasn't Bill's fault he was missing a toe and had a limp. He hadn't shot off his toe like some chicken shit draftee or reservist too gutless to face combat. Bill wanted to get shot at! To find out if he was really brave or not. Would he piss his pants, too afraid to move, or attack the enemy like a wild man? Firing his Government Issue machine gun and finding out what it felt like to actually kill somebody. Maybe even lots of somebodies. Not doing it like a bad guy though, but a good guy, like a real American hero.

But the Marine Corps, Army, Navy, Air Force, Coast Guard—even the National Guard—all turned him down. Nobody wanted him. Why the fuck not? Okay, so he wasn't book smart and didn't read good. So he limped a bit. So big fucking deal! The recruiters didn't think he could fight? Let 'em go ask folks who knew him if Bill Dunlop, Jr. was a fighter.

Dunlop a fighter? Oh yeah, man! You fucking better believe it, he is!

Bill's missing toe gave his walk a bit of a dip to his left was all, and sometimes threw his balance off some, but no fucking way was he crippled. He didn't need a cane or a wheelchair, did he? So why couldn't any of the stupid recruiters in their fancy uniforms with stripes and medals and shit all over them get their heads out of their asses long enough to give him a fucking chance?

But nope, they saw what they saw. They couldn't look into a man's heart and see the real him. The stupid pricks!

Like that other prick True Man who'd been at the Human Be-In at San Fran's Golden Gate Park. Got sky high there, man, oh yeah, he'd cop to it. It was wild, fucking something else, man! Of course being so cool he saw Bill as a harmless gimp, some dodo Bonnie picked up out of pity, but nobody you had to take seriously, man.

True Man had eyes for Bonnie from the start and Bill noticed that she might have eyes for him, too.

One evening he took True Man out back for a walk in the beautiful aspens where they had a heart-to-heart, after which True Man avoided Bonnie like she had the plague.

If Bonnie suspected anything about the cause of True Man's sudden loss of interest in her, she said nothing about it to Bill. But a couple of times he caught her smiling at him for no good reason, a sweet, kind of knowing smile, Bonnie cocking her head to one side and giving it a little shake, like *can you believe this man of mine?*

Even with True Man out of the picture, Bill thought it was nuts for them to think of staying in Colorado, and did his best to talk some sense into her.

"Lookit, woman. Here we are chugging back and forth to Boulder five days a week where lucky you gets to clean up tourists' crap in that shitty little locomotel for minimum wage and hardly ever a tip, 'less you count all those little soaps and shampoos you steal, and me getting to wear a tall white chef's hat and a sandwich board with 'Franco's Pizza, Best in Boulder' on the front and back. Gimping up and down Franco's block waving at traffic and grinning like some down and outer just soooo happy to wear a fucking sign eight hours a day. And for what? Diddly-squat, that's what! Turning over a bundle of cash and at the end of each day and getting paid in cash, a small folded wad of greasy bills, all ones to make it seem more than it really was."

"You don't like it," Bonnie had said, "go find something better." Like she meant just the job but her look telling him that went for her, too. Same thing she said if he complained about the way she treated him or some new guy he knew she was banging behind his back. Except for one time he'd never forget, he got about half a sentence of the same old same old complaint out of his mouth when she busted out bawling like a baby. She knew how terrible she was to him, she wailed. Really, she did! Billy was so good to her, he was such a prince of a guy, yet she treated him like shit. Though she really didn't want to.

"Really, Billy, I don't! But still ..." shaking her head, "I still do it, don't I? I know it's awful, yet I keep doing it. I'm just hopeless."

Wanting to make her happy, Bill tried bringing in more money and kept looking for something better. He had experience as a dishwasher and janitor and truck dock loader, but no one seemed to need him.

"You think I'm not busting my balls trying to make more money?" he asked her.

"No," she said, patting his knee. "I know you are."

Then one day he carried home a flyer from the pizza shop and told her he'd asked Mr. Franco could he please have the weekend off because his Mom and Dad were coming to visit and he hadn't seen them for years.

But Bonnie said he'd told her that his Mom died drunk years ago and that he'd never even met his Dad. Well, Bill said, right, the visit business was a lie but it was true he hadn't seen them for years so it was only half a lie, really. Anyhow, that wasn't the point.

And in return for the time off he had promised Franco he'd be back on Monday and work the whole day for half pay. Maybe Mr. Franco didn't much like it, but where else would he find somebody dumb enough to work so cheap—except maybe a wino who'd probably take the customers' cash, spend it on jugs of Dago Red and hole up somewhere to get blotto. Bill was no prize maybe but at least he was honest. Pretty much.

That Saturday Bill had Bonnie drive them out a gravel road headed nowhere.

"Where are we going?" she wanted to know.

But he kept his mouth shut until he said "Pull in there, that bar there."

The Frontier Tavern was a good old shit-kicker, blood-bucket roadhouse stuck in nowhere where Bill ended up getting both eyes blacked and his nose not broken but swollen pretty bad and pouring blood like a washer-less faucet. He had won three fights on Saturday, all by KO, and one by decision on Sunday, raking in twenty bucks for each win. Hell, if he still could've seen he'd have walked away with the Tough Man hundred buck jackpot, too.

On the way back to Ward, moving an ice-cube filled red bandana from one eye to the other, he counted their winnings.

"What the fuck is this? You didn't do what I told you to?"

"Baby, I should have listened to you, but ..."

"If you'd have bet half our cash like ..."

"I know. But I was afraid we'd end up broke. I thought I was looking out for us. Really, I did."

"What you should've done was believed in me. That's what you should've done."

She leaned over and gave his purpled cheek a quick peck. "Forgive me?"

He kept his trap shut. But, man, sometimes ...

Bonnie suddenly swerved off the road, bumping onto the narrow gravel berm.

"Shit!" Bill yelped.

She turned off the engine, yanked on the emergency brake and began unzipping his jeans.

"What're you doing? Somebody could hit us here, a truck or something."

He pushed her hands away, and again, but they kept coming back.

"Watch the rear view," she said.

Swiveling about to face him, she freed his stiffening dick.

"Bonnie!"

She dropped her head into his lap.

"Bonnie? Hey, sit up!"

"Shut up."

"You wanna get us killed?"

Then her mouth was on him and he couldn't talk. His body pressed back against the seat so hard he thought he'd bust it. When she was done she sat up and kissed him gently on his cheek, the smell of his seed powerful on her lips.

"Better?"

"I mean, Jesus Christ!"

"You feel better? Yes or no?"

"Yes, but ..."

"Good."

Back in central Ohio, Bonnie gunned the coughing bug down the two lane like she was trying to get to the apartment so quick that she didn't have to see the flat fields and dull towns along the way.

When they reached Olentangy, home to a Methodist college and a harness horse race track that drew bettors and their cash from nearby Columbus, Bonnie groaned like she was pain.

Finally, she turned onto Liberty Parkway, their street, which Bill was glad to see.

A bunch of neighborhood boys and girls ran wild in the grassy parkway and in and out of the street. A red-haired girl sat on a park bench and a boy, his back to her, stood shifting his stance from side to side, arms spread wide, eye darting about.

"Look out for the kids," Bill told Bonnie.

She pounded a fist on the horn, scattering them like chickens.

Then a red-haired boy came tearing across the street and Bonnie hit the brakes and horn—*Screech. Blat.* "Shit!"—with Bill stiff-arming the dash.

The boy slipped past the jailer, tagged the girl, yelling "Home free!" and the two of them ran off together. Brother and sister maybe, Bill thought, taking care of one another.

Bonnie stomped on the gas, the tires squealing like slaughtered pigs.

"Stupid brats!"

"They're just playing ringolevio," Bill said.

"I could've killed them. This neighborhood!"

"We played that a lot when I was a kid," Bill told her. "One side's the hunters, the other's the hunted."

Bonnie sighed.

"Your hunters grab your hunted, yell *one two three ringolevio* while they still got hold of them, and slap them in jail. But if one of your hunted—"

"Bill. Please."

"—runs in, dodges the jailer and taps the prisoner, yelling *home free*—"

"I'm not listening."

"—then you're home free. But if the rescuer gets tapped, one, two, three—"

"*Shut up.*"

"—Ringolevio, then he's in prison, too."

Bonnie swung into the curb and parked out front of a two-story red brick Victorian—probably a beautiful family home before the neighborhood went bad—where they rented the first floor, two bedroom, full bath apartment.

Getting out, she grabbed her purse and wrestled with the wheeled suitcase.

Bill hefted his duffle and the stuffed laundry bag with one hand and with the other picked up the cat carrier. The powder blue plastic cage was made for one cat, and Mick and Cher were packed in like cows in a cattle car. Tufts of gray fur and black fur stuck out the narrow air slots.

Bonnie jerked the suitcase free and headed up the walk, Bill following after.

Sweet Jesus, her swing and sway!

She fiddled with her keys at the door, then banged a fist hard on the metal storm. "Son of a bitch!"

Bill stood clear. She was really pissed now. Here she was, hating like hell to come back to Ohio and then getting locked out when she did.

The storm swung wide and a guy in boxer shorts and a wife-beater stood there.

"Bonnie baby!"

"Lester."

They gave each other a hug.

Lester was tall and well-built with black curly hair and a muffin-duster 'stache.

"How come you're all locked-up," Bonnie asked. "Got yourself a piece of honey cake in there?"

Lester laughed. "Baggie of grass is all. Don't want Johnny Law surprising me."

"Mm-hm." Bonnie giving him the x-ray eye.

"So who's this here?" Lester asked. "This your Billy?"

"Bill," Bill said.

"Bill?"

"Right."

Lester nodded. "Okay, then. Bill." Giving him a bored-ass look like Bonnie's, Bill was no more worth noticing than the cats or baggage. But when he'd first set eyes on Bill, Bill had caught the flicker of surprise in Lester's eyes. Maybe Bonnie hadn't mentioned Bill's size to him.

Then Lester followed Bonnie inside and Bill followed Lester.

Her bags dumped on the living room floor, Bonnie was in the kitchen filling the cats' water and food bowls. Bill knelt to let the Mick and Cher out of their cage.

Lester opened the fridge and took out a couple of beers, popped off the caps, handed a bottle to Bonnie and clinked his against hers.

"Business first," she said, taking a seat at the tiny kitchen table.

Bill moved from room to room, remembering how happy he and Bonnie had been there, despite their fights. Back in the kitchen he leaned against the fridge, watching Lester and her. Was he going to end up getting blamed for them coming home from the mountains too early? For the trouble that caused now with Lester's sublet? Probably. Like in Colorado when they got kicked out of Alicia and Jake's house. Though really that wasn't Bill's fault, even if he did forget to shut the door to their room and the cats got out into the house when Alicia had warned them up front the cats had to stay in the room because she was really, really allergic.

Okay, maybe getting kicked out was sort of his fault. Alicia's face all puffed up, red as a circus clown's. But Alicia had had it in for Bonnie Jo Pike from day one, what with Jake, Alicia's man, being one of Bonnie's old boyfriends. That was what ruined things there, really, Bonnie's coming on to him.

Sure, all Bonnie and Bill had had in their room was a sink and toilet, with the tub and shower being downstairs. What could you expect for dirt-cheap rent? Nobody but an old boyfriend would have given Bonnie such a great break.

And how come it was she always took her shower when Alicia was off to work and Jake, the writer, was home alone? Her sashaying out of the downstairs bath wrapped in a towel that barely covered her breasts and bottom and just happening to pass by the open door of his study.

Bonnie was always complaining about her ass being fat as a sow's and her tits flopping like water balloons, but she knew darn well that guys really liked how she looked. Bill sure as hell did and had told her so lots of times, but she'd only shake her head, saying, "Well, sure. *You*."

Jake had liked her looks, too. Anybody but a blind man could see that. But did he like *her*? Enough to stand up for her? When Alicia kicked them out, did he do anything but hang back and keep mum as a fucking mummy? Nope.

It was Bonnie got them into the place and Bonnie got them kicked out.

So, too strapped to afford anything else around there, Bonnie and Bill had to hit the road for home. Whose fault was that? Not Bill's; no way. He fucked up a lot but not that time. He had done nothing but try to *help* Bonnie. Like always.

Like now. Keeping his trap shut, not wanting to mess up anything, but ready to toss Lester out on his ass if he gave Bonnie trouble.

Bonnie proposed that she and Bill take the bedroom and its double bed and Lester take the sofa. Lester started to object but Bonnie cut him off. Of course he would get a reduction in rent. Say fifty percent, which Bonnie thought was—but Lester said hey, whoa, hold on there. They should split it equally between the *three* of them. That's what she was saying, Bonnie said, but Lester said no, babe, equal meant thirds not halves: Lester, Bonnie and Bill. Unless she was claiming Bill as a pet, like the cats.

Don't be a prick, she told him. But then she gave in, thirds it was.

That night Lester already had plans to stay at a lady friend's place, so Bonnie and Bill had the place to themselves. Bonnie seemed really happy to be home alone, just the two of them. She put on an Aretha Franklin platter and they cuddled on the sofa, humming along with "I Say a Little Prayer for You," Bill drinking a beer and Bonnie downing a couple of vodka tonics.

Then she took Bill to bed and fucked his brains out. He cuddled with her afterward, telling her how much she meant to him, but then saw that she was dead to the world and slid his arm from beneath her head and slipped out of bed.

He liked how peaceful she looked when she slept. It made him want to tuck her in like he was her father looking out for her. Though, she'd never said much about her father except that he was an office systems salesman always on the road and who, even when he was home, hardly noticed her. Her mother? She owned a flower shop where she spent tons of time.

One time when they'd been drinking pretty hard, Bonnie told Bill that when she was ten and her parents were off to Chicago for an office supplies convention, an uncle who everyone thought was such a prince of a guy volunteered to look after her and he raped her. He said that if she ever told anyone he would say she was lying. Everyone knew she told lies all the time (which was true, Bonnie admitted), and he'd say she had confessed to messing around with high school boys in cars.

But then another time she told Bill to forget she'd ever said anything about that uncle stuff. It was bullshit was all it was. It had never happened. It was a just a story she made up to get attention.

Sleepless, Bill sat in the dark kitchen, his mind wandering around like a lost hound.

In the glow of the streetlight through the front room bay windows he stared at his bare feet planted on the black and white linoleum. At the empty space where his left little toe should have been.

He swung his head from side to side like a cow shaking off horseflies.

When Billy's father took off for parts unknown, leaving Mom and Billy on their own, his mother had to work six nights a week, 5-11, waiting tables at Luna's Bar & Grill so they could pay the rent on their lousy apartment and not get stuck in the poor house, and be able to buy enough food at Bargain Mart to keep them from starving.

"I *have* to leave you home alone nights, Billy. It's not like I want to, but we can't afford a sitter. You know that, don't you? It hurts me bad to have to do it; it makes me feel like I'm not a good mother. But you're getting to be my big boy now, aren't you. Five already! Can you believe that? Won't be long now before you're in school and we'll have to find a way to pay for books and school clothes."

But she didn't want him to be scared nights. They had good strong locks and if some bum or burglar tried sneaking in through a window they were in for a big surprise. Weren't they, Billy?

Then came the night he kept hearing strange noises out front. Maybe it was just the wind because it was kind of windy out, but maybe not, maybe someone was trying to break in to kidnap him or kill him. He got out of bed, got the butcher knife from the kitchen and, moving slow and silent as an Indian brave, checked the back door, found it locked, and was going to check on the front when pain shot through him so bad he dropped the knife and fell on the living room floor crying and rolling around, hurting so bad he thought he was dying. His left little toe was clamped in one of the rat traps Mom set under the windows to stop burglars. Every time he tried to get up he ended flat on his back again, fighting to catch his breath.

He wanted to go for help but was afraid to. The crazy couple next door were always hitting each other with a rolling pin or breaking dishes on one another's head. The old war veteran upstairs hated all his neighbors and warned them he had lots of guns, kept them all loaded and knew how to use them.

Billy had pulled up a corner of the old blue bath towel Mom used as a floor mat and bit on it hard to keep from screaming. He was still on the floor chewing on the towel when he heard one of Mom's boyfriends talking outside the door. He thought maybe he was dreaming, but then she unlocked the door and came in and switched on the light.

God in heaven what had he gone and done now? She started to kneel beside him but lost her balance and sprawled sideways onto the floor. God *damn* it! Finally she got herself into a sitting position and went to work on his toe. But every time she almost had it free of the trap. Billy would flinch and she'd lose it.

"Lay still! How in hell can I get this goddamned thing off you if you keep twisting and kicking? Chew on your towel, Billy, and hold still. I'm only trying to help you."

When finally the trap was off, he could do nothing but curl into a ball and cry.

His mom patted his back and gave him a kiss on the forehead.

A little kiss, but a kiss

Why hadn't he put ice on it?

He didn't know.

Because that was the thing to do, she told him. You'd think anyone would think of that first thing. God, she hoped he wasn't retarded!

The next day he hadn't been able to walk without limping but she told him he'd get over it soon enough. But by the end of the week the toe was swollen purple and puss was coming out it. Mom didn't want to but said maybe they'd better see a doctor. But the doctor they always went to because he gave her a break on the bill said he couldn't help, not this time. They needed to see a surgeon, he said, and gave her a name and number. At the surgeon's he told her no, it couldn't wait, it had to be done right away and she had to pay up front in cash. She said she'd have go get the cash, took Billy by the hand and had started for the door when the surgeon picked up the phone and told her if she left with the boy he'd call the police and have her run in for child neglect. Mad as hell, Mom left Billy there and came back with the cash, and the man cut off Billy's toe.

Lucky for a change, Bill landed a job on only their fifth day back in town: night janitor at a big insurance company on the north side of Columbus only fifteen miles from Olentangy. His limp made no difference to them and there was a head janitor to show him what to do when and how to do it right.

After two weeks on the job, Bill got his first pay and treated Bonnie to dinner at a nice steak house and she said she was really happy for him. Though he knew she still was ticked off that last week without a word to her he'd gone and traded in his Harley for a new ride.

"A Nash Rambler?" she'd squawked. "A station wagon? That's a suburban mommy's car, for fuck's sake!"

Winter was coming, he'd told her.

At the steak house he had enjoyed seeing her look happy for a change. So he hadn't said anything about the bad parts of his new job. How the old head janitor picked on him for not working faster and called him dummy when Bill made a mistake. Bill had told the man to please call him by his given name, but the man wouldn't listen. It would serve him right if Bill taught the old fart a good lesson, but he was too smart for that. He didn't want to get slapped in jail for assault so he had a straight forward talk with the man and told him that the very next time he called his Bill "dummy" he would lose a good worker.

And then he did and so he did.

And on a Thursday night, damn it, one night short of Bill's second pay, and Bill didn't know if they'd give it to him or not when he went by the office on Friday like usual to pick up his check. They had to, didn't they? He'd earned it, hadn't he? They better not try to cheat him out of it, the fuckers!

Heading home he worried that he'd done the wrong thing. But it would be wrong to stay and let the man talk to him like that, wouldn't it?

He stopped at a Waffle House to think things out. The boney old counterman brought him a cup of coffee, took his money and gave him change without a word. Bill slid forward a quarter as tip and the man came back and took it.

There was nothing playing on the juke box and the coffee was strong and hot like Bill liked it. Two in the morning and the plastic booths were empty, but there were two other guys at the counter, one reading a newspaper, the other one smoking a cigarette and looking off somewhere, thinking about things maybe, maybe trying to think how to set things straight in his life.

Bill wrapped his big hands around the hot cup. No reason he had to tell Bonnie right away that he lost his job. First thing in the morning he could go out job hunting and, with any luck, might line something up quick and then just say he was switching jobs, that was all, better working conditions, a chance for promotion, something or other.

Parking the Rambler at the curb, he wondered if maybe he should just sleep in it and come morning go in like usual, like nothing bad had happened. Or go on in now and say they'd got done early tonight because ... why? Because the fire alarm went off! Right, and so they had to evacuate the building and then the fire trucks came and their boss showed up and said well, there was no sense in them just standing around so they could take off. And even though they hadn't gotten all their work done, he would pay them for half the night. Pretty good deal, hey Bonnie?

Not wanting to wake her and have to go through the whole business tonight, he slipped into the apartment as quiet as he could. But, as it turned out, nobody there was sleeping. He froze just inside the door, hearing them going at it, hot and heavy. He took slow, deep breaths, trying not to lose it. And on some level knowing, but only now admitting it to himself, that really it was nothing more than he had expected. Sooner or later, it had had to happen. He just hadn't wanted to face it, that's all; lying to himself to try to believe she wasn't lying to him. But now here it was. Behind his back and in his face.

He unclenched his fists. But what if it wasn't her fault? What if Lester had forced himself on her? Bill could be a hero, give Lester a whipping and kick his ass out for good.

Bonnie squealed like she did with Bill when she came.

Bill clapped his hands over his ears, trying to think things through—then found himself standing in the kitchen where the butcher knife lay on the sink board. His wallet was in his hands and he was counting out bills and putting them on the kitchen table and weighting them down.

He went to the bedroom and opened the door.

"Bill!" Bonnie cried. "Jesus Christ!"

White-eyeing Bill, bare-ass Lester tried to get up but couldn't free himself of Bonnie's leg lock.

The cats scurried beneath the bed

"I need to get something," Bill said, his voice shaky.

"Not now!" Bonnie said.

He brushed past the bed, trying not to look at them, swept his hanging clothes from the closet rod and caught up his duffel.

"Get out of here!" Bonnie shrieked.

Bill said, "My half of September and October's rent is on the kitchen table."

"Just go!"

"Under the Buddha."

He passed through the living room, stepped out onto the porch and shut the door. Halfway down the walk he held up. Had he heard Bonnie call his name?

Maybe. Maybe not.

He slid into the powder blue Nash Rambler wagon and keyed the ignition. Everything that was his was in it. The wagon was slow but big enough for him to stretch out and sleep in the back if he had to.

Or live in it, if he wanted to.

FIFTY BUCKS

Fazio, a hotshot promoter, was yelling at Pops about the lack of sparring partners. Though everybody knew that at Pop's Corner sparring, partners were the promoter and manager's look out.

Pops worked the punch mitts with Napoleon Fremont, a tall, rangy light-heavy who sported an 18-3-0 record with 11 KO's and was hoping for a shot at the title if and when old Archie Moore got over his whipping by Rocky Marciano and decided to defend his title.

"You hear me, old man?" Fazio called.

Pops sidestepped his fighter, tapping Fremont with a mitt to his ribs. The contender immediately tucked in his elbows to protect his body.

"Or you deaf?"

Pops lowered his mitts, signaling a break. A ranked contender in his time, he looked like he still might hold his own with the current lightweight crop, though he was seventy if he was a day.

Painted on the wall behind him was Pop's motto: *Don't you be looking for an excuse to lose.*

He looked at Fazio like a man surveying a clogged toilet. "Don't like it here, take your business somewhere else."

"Shit," Fazio hissed. "That's what I get trying to save a few bucks."

Pops took up again with Fremont, flashing the focus mitts for a jab, jab, right cross, left hook to the body, *pop pop whack whack*, Napoleon nailing every shot.

"That's it, son." Pops said. "Good work."

Fazio motioned to his bodyguard, gave him change and sent him to the house phone to see if they could dig up somebody to give Fazio's new boy, Killer Dick Kolvar, some rounds.

An aging heavyweight banged the heavy bag, slow but hard. His trainer called for left hooks, three in a row, down up down, then up down up,

"He can't block 'em all, Jack. You keep it up; you'll take away the Kid's legs, then get 'em on the ropes and take his heart."

Slumped forward on a bench against the wall, a bum watched the heavyweight thump the bag. A filthy turkey-shit green greatcoat hung from the watcher's rounded shoulders like a cape or a burial shroud. His head was covered by a woolen Irish cap so filthy and greasy it was black as motor oil. Every so often the man flinched and ducked his head as though someone were punching or shooting at him. He hugged himself and managed to sit still, breathing deeply. Then he straightened up, tipped back his head and drained the last of a bottle of muscatel wrapped in a paper sack.

Breathing hard, sweat-soaked, the heavyweight held out his hands to have the gloves pulled off.

"What the hell you think you're doing, Jack?" his trainer said.

"I'm done."

"What are you, joking? We still got an hour."

"Not today."

"We only got a week before Hogan ..."

"Yeah, and I'm as ready as I'm gonna get. For a man my age I'll look real good in there when Kid Hogan's bouncing me off the canvas."

He pulled on a jacket, put up the hood and headed for the door.

"What about your shower?"

"It's raining, remember?"

The trainer complained but followed his heavyweight out the door.

Fazio came to stand in front of the bum on the bench, looking down at him. The man didn't look up. When Fazio touched the bum's shoulder the man flinched and threw up his fists,

"Hey, hey! Take it easy, Haskins. How'd you like to make some money? Cash."

The bum lifted his face. His bloodshot eyes squinted, trying to focus.

"You too drunk to stand? Huh? No? Okay, here's the deal. My boy Kolvar needs a sparring partner. You used to be a pretty good fighter, right? Come give him a couple rounds, why don't you?" Fazio took out a fat wallet and laid two tens on the bench. "Okay? Just move around the ring a bit, help him break a sweat? He'll take it easy. What do you say?"

The man shook his head.

"Christ, you fucking bum." He lay down another ten spot. "*There.* Think of the joy juice you can buy for that."

The man shook his head again,

"God damn! What I gotta do around here to get some cooperation? Hey, Pops! You know this guy. Tell him I'm just trying to help him out, will you."

Pops glanced over, eyes resting a moment on the bum, and then turned away. "Man don't never listen to me."

Fazio hissed. He counted out three more tens, slapping them down on the bench one by one. "Fifty bucks? When's the last time you had that much cash? Think how long you can stay stewed on that."

Looking up, the man let out a heavy sigh.

"Yours for the taking."

The man picked up the five tens and rose from the bench. Walking to the ring he stuffed the money into a pocket of his overcoat.

"Pops," Fazio called. "How much to rent Haskins here some gear?"

"Don't need it," the man said. "Let's go."

"That's the spirit," Fazio said

Lucky Haskins shucked off the ratty greatcoat, dropped his cap on it, then took off a broken-down pair of boots and climbed into the ring in dirty sweat socks. Fazio's trainer laced him into twelve ounce gloves and moved to rub petroleum jelly on his face, but Haskins shook it off. "We're taking it easy, right?"

"Right," Fazio said.

"Two minute rounds, not three."

"You got it."

Haskins climbed clumsily into the ring and stood with his back to a corner post, facing Fazio's boy, a local Polish middleweight hard as rock.

Fazio's trainer set a round timer and waited, then rapped a drumstick against the gong mounted at ringside. *Ding.*

Lucky, gloves up, waited in the corner and let Killer Karl Kolvar come to him. They exchanged jabs, Kolvar's stiff, stinging. Lucky tried a right cross but it was slow and wide. His opponent feinted a right, and then uncorked a vicious left hook that missed taking off Haskins' head off by a whisker. Killer Kolvar backed off, shrugged his shoulders—"Oops, mistake, sorry." He came forward again and Lucky hunched, fluttered a jab in front of his man's eyes, and then put all his weight into an uppercut to the Killer's nuts. Kolvar hunched, gagging, and Lucky drove the top of his skull into Kolvar's face. Blood spurted from a gash above the left eye.

Fazio was screaming. "You fucking insane? Look what you did, you stupid fucking bum! He's supposed to fight next week! Jesus Fucking Christ! Duke!"

The bodyguard moved toward Lucky.

"Uh-uh!" Pop's called out. "No fighting in here 'cept in the ring."

The bodyguard held up. Pops allowed no guns in the gym except for the double-barreled 12 gauge he kept handy to keep the peace.

Fazio screamed at Haskins that he'd pay for this, he couldn't hide forever, they'd find him and when they did ...

Lucky Haskins took the five tens from his greatcoat pocket and tossed them to the floor. "Keep your money," he said, and walked away.

Outside, he turned his face up into the rain. It felt clean.

The Yellow Footprints

"Mind if I sit here?"

The Marine staff sergeant in starched, pressed tropicals, his tie knotted, his cap placed neatly beside him on the bar, took in the dumpy man at his elbow. After a pause, he said, "Help yourself."

"Thanks." The man climbed clumsily onto the stool at the far end of the bar, unzipped his blue windbreaker and propped a knobby blackthorn cane against the bar. "Free country, right?"

"It is."

"Didn't mean to crowd you any, but ..." He jerked his head in the direction of the booths packed with local college students loudly celebrating the start of spring break. "I want to be as far away as I can from spoiled brats drinking and drugging on daddy's dough." He raised a finger to the bartender, who came right over.

"Hey there, Ernie. The usual?"

"You got it, Butsy. And bring the staff sergeant here whatever he's having. On me."

The sergeant shook his head, "No sir, that's not necessary."

"Please. Any time I can treat a fellow jarhead, I do it."

"Well ... thank you."

When Butsy dropped off their drinks—a shot for the sergeant and a shot and a schooner of draught for Ernie—Ernie dumped the shot, glass and all, into the beer, swirled it about, glasses clinking, and announced "Depth Charge!" He held up the schooner to the sergeant. "Corporal Ernie Higgins," he said, "USMC retired."

The sergeant lifted his shot glass, "Staff Sergeant John Ryerson," and they tapped glasses.

A bearded boy on his way to the john glanced at them with disdain. Ernie hard-eyed him but let it go.

"I bought you that drink because I appreciate your service, Sergeant," he said. "And that's not just some 'thank you for your blah blah have a nice day' civilian bullshit neither. No sir, I'm a man who knows the score. All that fruit salad on your chest? I can see you're an old salt who's been around."

The staff sergeant dipped his head.

"How many tours so far?"

"Two."

"Mind me asking where?"

"Iraq. Desert Storm, 2003; Abu Ghraib, 2005."

Ernie grunted as if struck. "Hard duty. Yes, sir. I'd say you've earned some stateside time after that. You're a recruiter, right?"

The sergeant nodded.

"I kinda figured. A squared-away, good-looking Marine's Marine like you, you're a natural for the post. Bet you do a damn fine job, too."

"I do my best."

"A recruiting post ain't so easy, neither. I realize that. Not when you're trying to talk a bunch of teenage punks and college dropouts into manning up and doing something with their life."

"I wouldn't put it that way."

"Course not. 'Cause you seem like a nice guy. Course I guess you got to, being a recruiter. Me, I'm just a crusty old fart. 'Nam was my war. Graduated Parris Island in June and by January was dug in at Khe Sanh. What a cluster-fuck that was! Up on a hill out in the open, sitting ducks surrounded by tens of thousands of North Vietnamese."

The sergeant shook his head in sympathy.

The boy passed behind them again to take a seat in a booth packed with students.

"Our NVA kill ratio was out-fucking-standing," Ernie said, raising his voice, "Way the hell up in the thousands. Course, it's kinda hard to miss hitting a herd that size. Fucking gooks chewed us up pretty bad though. Four out of ten jarheads killed or wounded. Me, I lucked out. All I ended up with was a deaf left ear, a fucked-up back and an old age full of bad dreams and sleepless nights. But what the hell, eh? Only one thing you can count on in this life, Sergeant, you're not getting out of it alive."

Drunk or stoned, the bearded boy stood, pointed an accusing finger at the staff sergeant and announced "Peace is the answer, not war!"

His booth mates showed their support with hoots and lifted fists.

"Scrap the military!" he shouted, and his friends echoed him.

Ernie slid off his stool and took a step toward the booth.

"No, sir," the recruiter said, clamping a firm hand on his shoulder. "You do not want to do that."

Ernie held his ground for a moment, but then backed away. "Right, you're right."

The staff sergeant stood. "Let's go."

"I just got here."

"Yeah, well ..." He gripped Ernie's arm and led him from the bar through a chorus of catcalls and curses from the peace lovers.

Outside, Ernie yanked free, lost his balance and stumbled backward, dropping his cane and thumping hard against the bar's brick wall.

The recruiter retrieved the cane and dusted off the back of Ernie's jacket. "Easy, Corporal. We don't want the local law showing up."

Ernie smiled. "Not a good career move for you, right?"

"Absolutely."

"My apologies. I ... got a temper on me. Not the best thing, I know."

"Where's your car?"

Ernie jerked his head at the other side of the street. "That old boat of a Ford."

"Need some help getting there?"

"No, I can ... well, all right, if you don't mind."

The sergeant cupped Ernie's left armpit and, with the older man stabbing his cane at the pavement, they crossed Main Street and navigated the half block to the car. Ernie worked his keys, wedged himself into the driver's seat and asked where the sergeant was parked.

"The public lot by the post office."

"Best not to park the official ride out front a bar, right?"

The sergeant shrugged. "Thanks for the drink, Corporal."

"Hey, no! Come on, jarhead, I'll give you a lift."

"It's only a block or so."

"Five. Get in."

"Well ..." The sergeant slid into the car and Ernie fired up the engine.

"Open the glove compartment there, will you?"

"If you have a firearm in there I don't want anything ..."

"Nah nah, Sarge. Nothing in there but a pint of whiskey."

The sergeant looked in the box.

"Behind those packs of cigars there," Ernie told him.

"Right, I see it."

"Jack Daniels," Ernie said. "Black Label. And 'less I'm mistaken, that's what you were drinking."

The sergeant closed the box. "It was."

"And 'less I'm mistaken again you figured to have a few more if I hadn't shot off my big mouth and got our asses kicked out."

"Oh, no. Nobody kicked us out."

"Strategically retreated? Advanced to the rear?"

"Kept the peace."

"Roger that," Ernie nodded. "You know the seal's not even broken on that Jack."

"So I saw."

"Got it this afternoon. I like to keep a full one in there. Some nights I can't sleep, I take a drive and park out there along the Olentangy, walk down to the bank to sit and watch the water. Kick off my foot gear, stick my feet in the river, and take a few nips."

"Never been run in?"

"Hell, no! Not one D.U.I." He laughed. "The cops here all know Ernie Higgins. Solid citizen, annual donor to the Ohio Patrolman's Benevolent Association and a man who plays poker every other Wednesday at the VFW with the Chief of Police."

"Pretty sweet berth."

Ernie nodded. "Nothing I know more peaceful than seeing a river run by and having a drink or two."

"Can't argue with that."

"Hey, listen. Whyn't we head out there right now?"

"Kind of late."

"What, you got a curfew? Sit ourselves down by the water; tell war stories? I'm only up for one more shot, myself, so the rest is yours. What do you say, Marine?"

"Well, what the hell?"

Shoes off and pants cuffs rolled, Ernie leaned back on his elbows, his bare feet at ease in the cool flow of the river. The sergeant took another sip from the flask and offered it to him but Ernie shook his head. "Nope. Corporal Higgins has to drive back. So go on. Abu Ghraib?"

"Like I said, if I knew which desk jockey genius of an officer decided it was strategically important to hold a perimeter defense of that worthless shit box of a prison, I'd frag the bastard. We were taking heavy mortar and rocket fire, had waves of insurgents closing in, our close air support was an hour away, and we'd run so low on ammo that we fixed bayonets."

"In the shit!"

"Want to know just how damned desperate we were? We cheered to see Army National Guard units coming to support us. The Army? The fucking National Guard?"

"Ha!" Ernie said. "That kinda help, you're lucky to still be here. But like they say—only the good die young, right?"

Nodding, the sergeant stared at the water. Then, shaking off the memory, he offered Ernie the bottle. "Wanna finish this?"

Ernie sucked on a cigar. "No, I'm done."

The sergeant upended the pint, swallowed and coughed. "And afterwards, nothing's ever the same."

"Now if that ain't the truth," Ernie said. "Nothing is ever again the same." He pounded a fist on a knee. "I mean if that ain't the straight skinny goddamned fucking truth of it!"

The sergeant flipped the empty bottle into the river. It headed downstream, taking on water, but still was afloat as it passed from sight.

They sat in silence, heads down, and then Ernie perked up, singing in a raspy, off-key voice, "If I die on the Russian front." The sergeant joined in. "Bury me with a Russian cunt. Your left, your right, your left."

Ernie laughed. "Man, those old cadence counts! They start running through my head nights; I can't get rid of them. Come morning, I'm so beat I feel like I been on a fifty klick forced march in full battle pack."

The sergeant nodded. "I don't know but I've been told," he sang, Ernie adding "Eskimo pussy is mighty cold," the two of them joining on the chorus, "your lep, right, lep ..."

"Jesus," said the sergeant, "but we had a black drill sergeant from Kentucky who sang those cadences so damned sweet I swear he could make a dead grunt strut."

Ernie ground out his cigar on a rock and tossed it into the water. "I don't know but I been told—I'll be damned if that's not the story of a man's life. Just do what you're told, boy, son, Marine, shitbird! Which I did. Kept my ears open and my mouth shut and made buck sergeant at 21. Brought home the Vietnam Service Medal, a Combat Action Ribbon, Bronze Star, and a Purple Heart."

The sergeant nodded. "Semper Fi."

"Till the day I die," Ernie said.

They bumped knuckles.

"Kept them in a glass case on display right there in the living room. Something to take pride in, I guess. Though compared to my old man's record in World War II—the big one, he always called it—my haul wasn't all that much. He was as an artillery Captain in France and Germany. The Battle of the Bulge? It don't get any bigger or badder than that according to U.S.M.C. Captain Charles A. Higgins. He told my mother and me all about it, time and again. It used to drive me nuts. Now, though, I can understand it. Going to hell and back is something to be proud of and is goddamned hard to get off your mind. I know I sure as hell shot my mouth off about Viet Nam ever' damn chance I got." Ernie sighed. "My wife just didn't get it. Why couldn't I let it go, all that awful stuff had happened? Why did I have to keep on talking about it?"

"It's hard on a woman," the sergeant said. "Every one of my wives told me that."

"I'm going to the car, get another stogie. You sure you don't want one? I get 'em dirt cheap at the smoke shop I work at. Couple afternoons a week is all, something to keep me from going stir crazy in the house. They're seconds, but they ain't bad."

The sergeant shook his head.

"Be right back."

When Ernie returned the sergeant sat slumped forward, arms folded arms on his knees, head on his arms.

"Reveille!" Ernie barked, startling the man. "Drop your cocks and grab your socks, maggots!"

"Whoo. More tired than I thought."

"Brought you a cigar if you want one."

"No, thanks."

"Up to you." Ernie lit up, blew smoke. "Take a look at this."

"What the hell?"

"My old service pistol. I'm ashamed to say I reported it lost in 'Nam and sneaked it home in a ditty bag of shitty skivvies. For my money, they've never made a better sidearm than the 1911 Colt 45 semi-auto."

"Right. Put it away."

"Why?"

"We don't want somebody getting shot by accident."

"Nobody's going to get shot by accident."

"Not loaded, is it?"

"What the hell good's an unloaded gun?"

The sergeant scrambled to his feet. "Unload that weapon, Corporal! That's an order!"

Ernie racked the slide and pointed the .45 at the sergeant. "You're not my fucking commander!"

"Whoa! Okay, okay. Take it easy. But listen up now, you stay if you want, but I need to be getting back. Don't want to give me a ride, fine, I'll walk."

Ernie fired a shot into the dirt at the sergeant's feet. "Sit the fuck down, Staff Sergeant John Ryerson!"

The sergeant sat and stared back at him. "I don't know what your problem is but ..."

"Then whyn't you shut your trap and I'll tell you. My poor boy ..." He shook his head. "Nobody wants to hear about him."

"I'll listen. Okay? Sit down and tell me about it. Maybe it'll help get it off your mind."

"Fuck." Ernie sighed, and then lowered himself to the ground, legs akimbo, elbows on his knees, the .45 dangling at his crotch.

"So, what was his problem?"

Ernie shook his head. "What I ought to do is just forget about him and get on with my life."

"That's not bad advice, Ernie."

"No? It's what I kept telling his mother. But me, I can't do it."

"You talk to anyone about it?"

"Yeah. Bartenders."

"I mean a professional."

Ernie waved it off. "The kid never had a chance." He hung his head, shaking it slowly. "For starters, he was a goddamn simple wimp! That sounds pretty harsh, but really I loved my boy just like any father would."

"I'm sure you did."

"You're sure? Oh, thank you, Staff Sergeant Ryerson, you have no idea what that means to me!"

"I only meant ..."

"Shut the fuck up and hear me out. I loved him even though he drove me up the goddamn wall. I mean, what the hell kind of a boy is happy to sit home with Mommy all day watching TV, drinking soda pop and eating corn chips? Like he was an old fart with his life behind him. You are a young man at the start of your life, I told him. So act like it, for Christ's sake."

"You get him straightened out?"

"Nah. No matter all I did for him, and I hate to say this about my own flesh and blood, but he was hopeless. A loser from the get-go."

"Sorry to hear it."

"For one thing the wife had to give him a pussy name, Timothy, after her father the accountant. Dullest man you'd ever meet. Gray suit, white shirt, dark tie, trifocals, dentures so white they looked like plastic.

"The boy graduated high school okay but then didn't know what to do with himself. Went looking for jobs but said he couldn't find anything, so sat home with his mama watching TV. I told her it was no good for him. She said for me to quit picking on him, like it was okay if he stayed a baby. So I called up a cousin of mine ran a package delivery service. He owed me a favor from the time I went in and squared away a driver who'd been giving him lip. My boy needed work? Heck yes, he'd take him on.

"I made Tim give it a try; told him he might like it. He'd wear a uniform with a matching cap and an official-looking name tag pinned on the shirt. Would be driving all over Columbus, get to know the city, probably meet girls. Women went for a man in uniform, I said, his old man knew that for a fact. So, okay, he tried it. And maybe did his best, I don't know, but never managed to get the hang of navigating the city. Spent half his day lost and left half the packages at the wrong address. Wasn't long before my cousin called to say he didn't owe me that much and was letting the boy go.

"The wife liked it fine, having her boy back home. If I said he needed to be out on his own, she'd say he was good company, a real comfort to her, unlike some people she could name.

"Then after he was gone, the wife who used to go on and on about my drinking and not sleeping, letting the war get me down like I was some kind of weakling, not a real man—how did she handle it? Let herself fall apart, that's what. Ended up on all kind of meds for her nerves, her heart, her weight. Stuffing her face morning, noon and night, poor soul. She just couldn't suck it up and go on after losing her boy."

"He left home?"

"He died."

"Oh. Sorry. How?"

"In his sleep, poor kid. I hate to say this about my own blood, but he was a loser from the get-go. But of course, to my wife, I was to blame. I put too much pressure on him. After that, she wouldn't listen to a word I said. Wouldn't let me touch her. Looked right through me like I wasn't there. It was all my fault, she said. I had to be the big hero that her boy could never live up to. I kept telling her no, I never once told him he should follow in my footsteps. Fact is, I told him just the opposite. Not to. He just wasn't cut out for it, he couldn't hack it."

"Hack what?"

"The Corps. What the hell you think I been talking about?"

The sergeant opened his mouth and then shut it.

"He'd brought up the subject with me about joining up and seemed surprised that I wasn't clapping him on the back and congratulating him. Not that I didn't appreciate him wanting to please his old man, I told him that, but the fact was he just did not have what it took to be a Marine, much less than ever to face combat. But that was okay. He should just accept it and get on with his life. Teach school, be a priest, sell insurance; anything but the Corps.

"After our talk I heard nothing more about the Corps and thought that was the end of it. But no. He confessed to his mother it was something he really, really wanted to do and made her promise not to say a word to me until he was already on his way to boot camp. The whole thing worried her, but she didn't have the heart to forbid him to do it, or to break her promise to not tell me. So now he's dead."

"Combat related?"

"You kidding? Boot camp."

"The rifle range?"

"No, but that would have been the way to go, blow out his brains by 'accident.'"

"So it was accidental."

"Fuck, no, you dumb turd. I said that would have been a good way to go. In the line of duty. But the kid was too honest to fake it. I got to hand him that. No, he killed himself in the barracks."

"Jesus! I'm sorry to hear it."

"Why? Suicide may be a coward's way out, but it's a hell of a lot more honest than accidentally shooting yourself in the foot for a quick ticket home. No, honest Tim, God love him, his third week in, having fucked up from the word go and gotten pegged as a shitbird loser with no chance of graduating and so faced with being sent back to a fuck-ups make-up platoon to start the grind all over again from day one, after lights out he slipped his combat knife from its sheath and under his blanket slit both wrists.

"Jesus."

"Never made a sound—no scream, no grunt, not even a whimper. Nothing for his bunk buddy or the fire-watch duty to hear and report. Just laid there quiet and bled to death. You think that doesn't take guts! Come morning reveille sounds, the grunts hit the deck to form up and hey, there's a hole in the ranks. The D.I. checks Tim's rack and the shit hits the fan. Goddamn, what a lousy thing to have on your record. No D.I ever wants that. He didn't know the kid was section eight. What the fuck was the boy doing there if he had no chance of making it? Which was exactly what I'd tried to tell Tim!" Ernie sighed. "So that's it. End of Story. Son gone. Wife off the deep end."

"Man, I really ..."

"Feel my pain? Gee, thanks, Sarge. Afterwards his mother tells me that Timmy had seen a Marine recruiter to get information on joining up, came home and talked to her about it, but then had second thoughts, and she thought that was an end to it.

"And then, she said, the recruiter called the house to talk to him. Told Tim how proud his Marine vet father would be of him joining up. Tim liked the recruiter he told his Mom; he took Tim seriously, talked to him man to man. So he came back in to see you."

"Me? We have other staff ..."

"Staff Sergeant John Ryerson, he told his Mom. You got another recruiter in town name Ryerson?"

"No. But ... I don't remember him. I see a lot of ..."

"Well, like I said, he wasn't a very memorable boy. Kind of vague, floaty-like. His mother and I always had a hard time knowing what interested him, what he wanted to do. He sort of ... drifted around. Just shy, maybe. Or maybe a bit retarded. Whatever, he wouldn't have made much of an impression on you. He didn't make one on anyone. Looking through his high school yearbook could break your heart. No sports or clubs listed under his spaced-out graduation pic. Not a single student note or autograph front or back. Just fucking pathetic.

"I mean, if I told him once, I told him a hundred times: show some spirit, buckle down to work, make something of yourself. Then he starts talking about joining the Corps. Guess maybe 'cause my father and I'd been gung-ho jarheads. But I leveled with him right off. He'd dropped out of Boy Scouts, remember? He'd never played any sports. To my knowledge he never got any exercise. He read and ate and slept, that's all. So why in God's name did he think he'd have a chance in the Corps?

"Face it, I told him, you are not Corps material. The Few, the Proud? Right. And you can damn well bet they mean the damned few, too. Why is it you think most guys join the Army or Navy? Because they know they can't hack it in the Corps. But that's okay. No shame in knowing your limits. You hear what I'm telling you, son? If you're dead set on joining something, check out the National Guard. They do good work and generally stay close to home. Nice uniforms, pay's not bad, what do you say? But, no, he wouldn't listen. It was the Corps or nothing.

"Then it was nothing, I told him. I laid down the law. No Marine Corps for him. And no more talk about it, not a word. That was it!

"So, okay, he sulked around the house then, wouldn't talk to me, wouldn't look at me, had his poor mother worried sick. Ignore it, I told her, he'll come out of it. Just give him time.

"Then, a couple weeks later, on the day before he left for P.I., he told his mother he'd enlisted and was going and made her swear to God not to tell me until after he was on the bus. When I got the word I blew my fucking stack! She let the boy join the Marines? What was she, an idiot? She thought she was crying now? Wait till they shipped him home in a box.

"But she thought it would be best for the family, she said. When the recruiter called him and left a message, he'd said that Tim graduating P.I. would make his father proud of him. Would show his dad that he was a grown man now, and a fellow marine."

Ernie stopped to take a deep breath. "Okay," he said. "Get up."

"Now. Listen ..."

"Do it!"

The sergeant stood, warily, doing his best not to show fear.

"Look at you." Ernie said. "Not even shaking. Good man. Sarge. Now walk out into the water."

"What are you going to do?"

"Go stand in that fucking river!"

"Okay, okay." The sergeant stepped gingerly off the bank, moved a few feet, then turned, his hands spread to show his obedience. "See? No problem. But listen to me. You kill me and end up in prison, what's going to happen to your poor wife?"

Ernie shrugged. "Nothing. She's dead."

"But ..."

"Last week. Squad rushed her to Coronary Care but she was D.O.A."

"The poor woman."

"Ha! Best damn thing for her. She was miserable. I made her miserable."

"Okay, look. You're all torn up right now. You need time ..."

"Shut up and listen up. 'Death is nothing. But to live defeated and inglorious is to die daily.' Who said that?"

"What?"

"In history. Who said it?"

"I don't have any ..."

"Then guess, goddamnit it!"

"I ... Commandant Chesty Puller?"

"Shit, no! Napoleon Bonaparte. Every damn military man should know that. The great French general and emperor who sacrificed hundreds of thousands of his troops in wars to prove his immortal greatness? So courageous, so glorious! The stunted little fuck! So what's he do when he finally loses? Falls on his sword? Accepts public execution? Oh, no! He weasels a deal to get exiled on an island. The gutless coward."

"Ernie, I understand how ..."

"Don't come up here. Stay right where I put you."

"Listen to me. You don't want to do something you'll regret for the rest of your life."

"Regret for the rest of my life? Jesus Christ, haven't you heard a goddamned thing I said? My boy killing himself? You think I won't have to regret that for the rest of my fucking life? You shit-for-brains phony!"

Without hesitation, Ernie turned the .45, stuck it in his mouth, and pulled the trigger.

Hard Rolls

Mom got home around eight, and she and Billy ate their supper then at a card table in the living room that was Billy's bedroom too. At the Division Street apartment there had been room for all three of them to eat in the kitchen, but the new place on Rosewood was small. It was just the two of them and they did okay.

He always waited to eat his supper with her. She said he didn't need to, but he did. They ate in the Rosewood apartment's big room, usually something from the Pick Me Up Cafe. Tonight it was potato soup, ham slices and hard rolls. Mr. Stahl was good about letting her take home food too old to serve, Mom said, though Billy thought maybe she stole it. If she did, you couldn't blame her. On her own now, she had to look out for herself and her son. And, not being raised Catholic like Dad and Billy, she didn't know that lots of everyday things you did were mortal sins. Every chance he got, Billy lit vigil lights at St. Joseph's for the intention that Mom would be saved. When he didn't have change, he wrote down what he owed and tried to make it up later.

Last fall when they had all the trouble on Division Street, he had been trying to sleep when he felt someone sit on the side of his bed. A heavy weight, his dad. He kept his eyes closed and his breathing slow and even.

"This is just between us," his dad whispered. He smelled of beer. "I'm not gonna get mad, not if you give it to me straight."

Billy puffed out his lips as he breathed.

"Don't try to con me, you're not asleep."

He popped open his eyes like he was just waking up. *What?*

"It wasn't your mother saw me coming out of the Tap Room tonight, it was you."

His bedroom door was open and the hall light on but his dad was leaning over him and Billy couldn't make out the look on his face.

"You were out sneaking around when I told you to stay home."

Billy shook his head.

"Bull. I *know* you're the one. But see, what you don't know is, that lady I was with, she knows a guy who maybe can get me a job. You see what I'm saying? She's not my girlfriend. But that's what your mother thinks now. Because you told her."

"No, Dad."

"I already know you did it; I just want to hear it from you. I won't tell your mother you said anything. Scout's honor. What do you say?"

The trouble with Dad was that you couldn't tell what might make him happy or mad. When he and Mom fought it almost always ended with her screaming *I never know what you want from me!*

"Come on, spit it out. She doesn't walk home that way, not anywhere near the Tap. You had to be the one."

"No," Billy said.

"She never saw me herself, did she?"

"I stayed home, I did my homework."

"All she's got is what you told her, right?"

"And then I listened to the radio, *The Lone Ranger.* She was already mad about something when she got home but didn't say what."

"Shut up and listen. Just tell her you made a mistake. Come on. I'll owe you one."

"But I *didn't* tell her anything."

"You thought it was me but turned out it wasn't."

"I don't even know what you're talking about."

"Mistaken identity. She'll believe you; you know she will. What do you say, partner?"

"Dad, I'm not lying. Really, I'm not!"

His dad had pushed off the bed hard and gone to the door. In the hall light his face looked more disappointed than mad. "Okay. You take care of yourself," he said.

After supper Mom did the dishes in the tiny kitchen while Billy sat in the big room and sorted her tips. She had the radio on and hummed along a bit with Perry Como's "Don't Let the Stars Get in Your Eyes" and the Ames Brothers' "You You You." She didn't cry as much anymore and so Billy thought maybe she was happy.

He flattened and smoothed out dollar bills to slide into a bank envelope. Had he done what he was supposed to and stayed home while Mom worked and Dad went out to see a guy about a job, they'd still be a family. But no, he had to go out and hunt for coins along the curb by the bars. The second he spotted his dad coming out of the bar, he ducked behind a parked car. A red-haired lady held Dad's hand as they walked away.

Mom could tell that something was wrong that night the minute she walked in and she'd kept at him and at him until he broke down and told her. He cried, begging her not to tell Dad, and she promised not to. She hugged him and said he hadn't done anything wrong. He'd told the truth; he was a good boy.

Billy packed the counted coins into the brown roll wrappers. At school sometimes he took things if no one was watching, and in stores too. Nothing big: lunch money, candy, gum. Even Holy Cards sometimes. But he never took as much as a penny for himself from Mom's tips and knew she'd be proud of that. He'd *borrowed* some, but only once. An eighth grader was picking on him and other sixth grade guys, and so Billy took a roll of nickels to use after school and when he was done with it had put it back with Mom's tips. He never told her what he did. She'd only worry. It was better if she didn't know.

WATCHMAN, WHAT OF THE NIGHT?

At 3 a.m. Travers stood his push broom against a wall and went downstairs to the Family Bargain discount department store's lunch counter. Henry already was seated at the counter, hunkered down over his lunch. Short and squat, Henry looked like a toadstool.

Travers took his American Bulldog .38 short from its leather holster and laid it on the counter. He sat and opened his black metal lunch box, taking out the coffee thermos and a wax paper-wrapped cheese sandwich.

Henry mangled a tomato with his gums, juice and seeds dribbling from his chin onto a paper towel. His dentures sat on the counter like a disembodied grin.

"How come you don't use those things?"

"Don't fit right."

"Get new ones then."

"Costs dough, kiddo."

Travers swiveled his stool away from the old man. He bit off a chunk of sandwich. A big mirror occupied the wall at the end of the counter. He grimaced at his image in the drab gray pants and shirt. He hated having the name tag, *Art*, pinned over his left breast pocket. What did he need a name tag for when the only person he saw from 11 p.m to 7 a.m. was Henry?

At 68, Henry had ended up in such a shitty minimum wage janitor/watchman job, six nights a week, 10 p.m. to 7 a.m. because it was all he could get. At 20, Travers hoped to hell the same wasn't true of him. He saw it as a temporary situation. Although he'd put up with it now for nearly ten months, he felt that at any time he wanted he could go out and land something better, more permanent, just like he'd moved up from greasy spoon dishwasher to watchman. Maybe next he'd get into sales of some kind. Or over the road trucking, get to see some country.

But so far, he'd not been able to come up with anything he wanted to do for the rest of his life. Every week he put money away, saving up a nest egg. He might just take off to California—San Diego, maybe, where two of his high school buddies worked as hospital orderlies. Carrying bedpans for the living dead couldn't be any worse than spending your nights with a living dead coworker.

Travers unscrewed the top of his thermos and poured black coffee into its cap cup. From the All-Nite Diner across the street, it was strong and bitter but kept him awake and that's all he asked.

Usually about this time he'd slip into an office and phone his girlfriend, Joyce, a night attendant at a rest home in east Toledo, but last month he'd told her that if all she could talk about was their getting married and having a kid right away, then there was no sense in them talking. He guessed she thought he was bluffing, but by now she knew different. Still, he kind of missed her.

His sister Barb, who seemed happy to type forty hours a week downtown at Dun & Bradstreet where everyone got to dress nice, was against him leaving town, saying Mom and Dad would miss him. But he couldn't see it. They were too caught up in their own troubles—the crowded apartment, Dad not able to hold a steady job, Mom sneaking around with the neighbor's husband—to miss Art. With him gone, it'd be just one less problem for them.

Henry mopped his face with the paper towel, folded his brown bag to stow in a pocket, and relit the stub of cigar.

"Those things stink."

"Yeah, I know."

"You're killing your lungs, you know that?"

"You get my age, so what? The kids grow up and take off. The wife's always down with female troubles." He puffed smoke. His fat ass hung over the stool. Angling from a back pocket was his Hi-Standard .22 semi-auto.

"Whyn't you get a holster for that pea-shooter?"

"Nag, nag. Just like the old lady."

"I'm just saying. You're going to drop that thing some night and shoot yourself in the ass."

"Know what I wish?" Henry said.

"Or, just my luck, *me*."

"I wish you'd call your girl, ask her out. That's what she's waiting for; that's the way women are."

Travers shook his head.

"You get back with her maybe you'll quit picking at me."

The rounded slump of Henry's shoulders reminded Travers of his father, a disabled vet who stayed cooped up, stuck in the apartment wearing an afghan over his shoulders like an Indian's blanket.

"Sorry," he said, "just trying to help." He sipped his coffee. "I mean I can find you something decent, cheap. Say at least a .32. Holster, too. Be happy to do it."

Henry gave Travers an appraising look and nodded. "Mighty white of you, but this one's okay."

"It's a *target* pistol, Henry!"

The old man stood and picked up his teeth. "Gonna take the rest of my break over in furniture. In peace and quiet, okay?"

He shuffled off in the brown corduroy slippers he insisted on changing into when he came to work.

Travers shook his head. If he was that broken down when he turned sixty he'd take the Doctor Smith & Wesson cure, swear to God.

He drained his coffee, rewrapped the unfinished sandwich, put it and the thermos back into his lunch bag, and headed up to sweep the second floor.

He guessed Henry meant well, but the poor old guy didn't know the first thing about being ready for trouble. Any more than he did about how bad Joyce wanted to be a mommy and how bad Travers did not want to be a daddy.

When you came right down to it, old Henry didn't know diddly-shit.

By four-thirty Travers had finished in appliances and was working toys. Scattering the pine-scented red waxed sawdust before him, he swept it slowly down the wooden aisles between shelves lined with plastic machine guns, plastic cowboys and Indians, wind-up race cars, battery-operated tanks, dolls of all kinds and sizes, doll baby buggies, rubber balls, plastic bats. Good thing about working nights was not having to be in the store when it was packed with shoppers: Papa with his beer gut, Mama with her hair in curlers, the brats grabbing at everything and squalling when they couldn't have it. He couldn't believe the amount of "Made in Taiwan" junk people tossed in their carts when their clothes looked like they came straight from Goodwill.

The first squeak he heard without really registering it; the second he thought maybe was the building settling. But there were more. He stopped, stared at the ceiling and listened. *There.* Like somebody walking on the third floor, the office floor. *But who?* Doors closed at ten and the supervisors and sales clerks were gone by ten fifteen. Nobody should be up there now. It sure in hell wasn't Henry; he never climbed stairs.

Travers laid down the broom and took out his pistol.

Four months on the job and not a bit of trouble. Like the first few months with Joyce. Maybe now all his troubles were coming at once.

The footsteps moved across the floor to the stairway. Travers backed quickly but quietly away, taking cover behind the nearest row of shelves. He palm was sweaty against the pistol's plastic grips. For the few extra bucks, he should've put on non-slip rubber grips.

Too late now to go down and get Henry to help. By then the burglar, if there was one, could go down the back stairs and out the door, or even out a window onto the roof and slide down a drainpipe.

Damn.

He slid aside a clutch of fuzzy pink cats and blue dogs and laid his arm across the shelf to steady his aim. *Is the robber armed? Who the heck would break into a place with two guards and not be armed?*

He thumbed back the .38's hammer, locking it in place. He told himself to aim at a leg, that could stop a man without killing him. But it was pretty dim by the stairwell, and the appliance section beyond it was completely dark. The torso was what cops went for.

A stair creaked. Sweat trickled into Travers' eyes. He blinked to clear them. Tried to keep his breathing even. Then the stairway was occupied and the figure left the stairs, coming out on the second floor. A medium-sized man, looked like. Dark clothing. Maybe a mask? Hard to tell. A gun in his right hand? Something. Travers squinted but couldn't tell what. The figure turned away from toys and crouched by the far wall. Travers sighted dead-center on its back. He felt he could sense the man's fear run like an electric current up along the barrel of the .38 to Travers' sweaty hands.

His index finger took up the trigger slack. The man moved soundlessly off between the ghostly white refrigerators and freezers to the rear stairway

When he could no longer see any movement, Travers relaxed his grip and eased down the .38's hammer. He stood breathing for a bit, and then went down the front stairway.

Henry snored in a Lazy-Boy. Travers shook his shoulder and the old man jerked up. "What? I'm awake!"

The .22 was wedged in the gap between the chair's seat and back. Travers reached in and retrieved it. "Forget it. It's all over."

"I'm awake! What is it?"

"We got robbed."

"*What*? Oh, Jesus. No!"

"Just now. Let's check the doors. I'll get the back, you check the front."

The back door was unlocked. Travers locked it and went up to the front where Henry stood, gun in hand, peeking out at the parking lot.

"It was locked," he told Travers.

"Right. The back was the one."

"This can't happen. They'll fire me!" Henry's dentures clicked. There were tears in his eyes. "Where were you anyway? Listen, Artie, we got to stick together on this. Don't say anything about my, you know, resting. Okay?"

Travers nodded.

"And I'll keep mum about your door being the one unlocked."

"Sure." Travers sighed. "I'll call Mr. Brock."

*   *   *

Five minutes after the cops got there, Mr. Brock showed up. He interrupted the sergeant questioning Travers and Henry. "What the hell were you two doing? Sleeping? Playing poker? All you characters are the same. I pay good money and I can't trust you to do the job right without watching over you all the time."

"He came in so quiet," Henry said. "He must've been a professional. One of those cat burglars you hear about it."

"Rummies and bums, the bunch of you."

Travers stared at Brock but kept his mouth shut.

A police sergeant reported that the back door had been jimmied and the lock bar taped back. The safe looked intact, but a cashbox had been pried open.

Brock threw up his hands. "Oh, great! That's all we need!"

"This one here," the sergeant said, nodding at Travers, "says he saw somebody go down the back stairs."

"You *saw* him? Then why didn't you *stop* him?"

"He was too quick," Travers said. "I couldn't get a … a hand on him."

"Why didn't you shoot him?" Brock said.

"What? You ever give us guns? Uniforms, right, but no guns." He glanced at the sergeant. "I'm not even sure if it's legal for us to have guns in here. Is it, officer?"

"If you don't have one, what do you care?"

"I don't," Travers said. "Just that Mr. Brock is saying I *should* have had one." Travers turned to Brock. "You didn't want me to maybe be breaking the law, did you?"

Brock fumed. "No. I'm a respectable businessman, officer."

"What about you?" the sergeant asked Henry.

"He's over sixty," Pat said.

"You have a gun?"

Henry looked to Travers. "No. Sir."

"One hundred and eighty dollars in that cashbox," Brock said. Hands on his hips, arms akimbo, he lowered his head, slowly shaking it from side to side, a man in pain. It struck Travers that the manager was enjoying the attention his dramatic anger earned him. "One hundred and eighty dollars!"

Brock broke off, looking up at Henry and Travers. "And you two. You thinking this is just going to blow over? Right, I should've put it in the safe, but I figure, hey, I got two guards here, what's the worry?"

"Mister Brock," Henry said. "We wasn't ..."

"You shut up. I don't want to hear another word out of either of you. I've got a good mind to fire you both right here and now!"

"Mister Brock," Henry started.

"Shut up. Just shut your mouth."

Henry studied the floor.

"And you," Brock said, turning on Travers. "I want ..."

"Mr. Brock," Travers said, smiling politely, "I can't speak for Henry, but as far as I'm concerned, you can stick this job up your royal ass because I quit."

"*Who* do you think you're talking to?"

"And you keep yelling at me, I might do it for you."

The police sergeant held up a hand. "Take it easy, son."

In the employee's locker room Travers stripped off the hated uniform and tossed it on a bench. He put on his jeans, shirt and shit-kickers, slammed shut the locker, and left the lock hanging open from the hasp with the key in it.

He waited for Henry out front in the parking lot. The old man shambled over, shaking his head. "Nothing like this has ever happened to me," he said. "I'm a family man, been a hard worker all my wife. Ask anybody knows me."

"Life," Travers said.

"What?"

"All your *life*. You said wife."

"Oh Jesus, will you take this seriously. We could lose our jobs."

"Not me. I quit."

"I get fired, it goes on my record. You get a bad record, who's going to hire you?"

Travers unlocked his Chevy's trunk, called Henry over and slipped him his pistol. "Stick it in your pocket, don't let it show." His own gun he left in the lunch bag wadded up in the spare tire well. He shut and locked the trunk.

"Well," Henry said.

"Yeah. Well."

He watched the old man get into his station wagon and head out of the lot and into the stream of traffic on Monroe Street without getting into an accident. Then he fired up his Chevy and hit the road.

Mother's Day

Mel parked her Chevy beater in a visitor's space, got out and stretched, exhausted and aching. Stupid to drive twenty-two hours straight in the middle of August with your A/C on the fritz, taking only three rest stop breaks to hit the toilet and catnap for twenty minutes on the front bench seat, cell phone alarm set, doors locked, windows cracked only an inch and Mace in hand, but she didn't want to waste any more time on the trip home than absolutely fucking necessary.

Though her mouth felt dry as dust, she lit up a cigarette, steeling herself for the ordeal, and sucked in nicotine down to the stub, which she flicked onto the blacktop.

Her plate was the only out-of-stater in a line of Ohio ones. Sunshine Florida, Buckeye nut Ohio.

Well, the sooner she got it over with, the sooner she could bed down at some cheapo loco motel and be back on the road by morning. She started off, but turned back to open her car and hide the Walmart bag beneath the passenger seat so somebody didn't smash a window to get at it. Whenever she made her guilt trip home, the first thing she did when she hit Toledo was to buy presents for her boys. This time it was a Rubik's Cube for Brody, her eight-year-old, and for five-year-old Chase the card game Uno. If she waited until after visiting the home she was afraid she'd be too upset to think of anything else. And tonight she'd be sure to call from the motel to wish them sweet dreams, even though that meant she'd have to ask their asshole father to put them on the line.

At the front entrance she picked up the intercom and said it was Melissa Carr for Ruth Michaels. She hated her married name but had kept it rather than chance confusing her boys or making them feel abandoned. No matter the bitterness she felt toward her ex, she took care never to speak negatively about the prick in front of her sons. She wanted them to feel wanted and in no way the cause of their parents' troubles.

One of the always-smiling Nigerian women staff came to the door and welcomed her in. Although Mel hadn't been in the home for the past three years, it looked like nothing had changed. Halls and lounges were filled with the living dead in wheelchairs and with walkers and canes. Most seemed zombies but some looked at her hopefully, as if she might bring their release. Like cats and dogs at an animal shelter.

Never would Mel let herself end up in such a hopeless limbo. Not as long as she had scripts for painkillers and sleeping pills. Making do with fitful naps and putting up with migraines for a week or so would be small price to pay for a painless way out.

After she signed in at the front desk, Mel was passed on to a second attendant who smiled kindly and said, "This way, please."

Her warm and soothing voice had a musical quality to it and Mel followed her like a child on the heels of the Pied Piper.

She wondered if the woman sang bedtime lullabies to the childish seniors. What a sweet feeling that must be, Mel thought. She herself had no memories of ever being sung to sleep. Told to sleep, yes. "What in Heaven is wrong with you? You want to keep your father and me up all night?"

One of her various know-it-all therapists had cautioned that memories could be twisted and falsified by emotion. *Yeah, maybe.* But Mel wasn't about to be talked out of what she knew she knew.

The cocoa-skinned woman led her down a long hall to a room at the very end. A rare single room, the cost of which was eating up any inheritance Mel might have hoped for. But who was she kidding? She had no doubt that, despite being an only child, she had been written out of the will the day after her father's burial.

"Your lovely daughter Melissa has come to see you," the attendant crooned to the sheeted form in the railed bed. "Can we open our eyes? Ruth? You have company."

Mel's stomach turned at the sight of her scarecrow mother, her denture-less mouth gaping, snoring loudly. For a moment she had to turn away. Why in God's name was she being kept alive? Everyone knew there was no hope for her. It would be a blessing if she just never woke up again. For her as well as everyone else. Although the thought of it sandbagged Mel with a load of guilt. That was what she wished for, wasn't it? Not for her mother's relief, but for her own?

"She just needs time to wake up," the attendant said. "If you talk to her she will come around. We just need to be patient,"

She patted Mel's arm and left the room.

Mel sat looking her mother's wasted body. If she hadn't already known who it was, she'd have taken her for a stranger.

"Hi," she said, laying a hand on a boney shoulder. "Mom? Hello. It's me, Melissa."

The old woman's utter lack of response hit Mel surprisingly hard. She realized she had never been anything much in her mother's view, but now it seemed she was nothing at all. Although why that should bring pain made no sense. How could she fear a loss of identity in her mother's failed memory when that identity was just what she had spent most of her adult life denying?

She dropped into the bedside chair. Glancing at the wall clock, she saw she had been in the room for six and a half minutes. You really couldn't leave in less than an hour. What sense did it make to drive over forty hours round trip to just duck in, glance at the breathing cadaver, and then split? You'd spend more time than that viewing the corpse at a funeral home.

Mel forced herself to reach out and take her mother's hand. It had no more substance than a dried leaf and she released it. She took the plastic pitcher from the bedside table, poured some water into her mother's glass, and drank it down.

Leaning back in the visitor's chair, she closed her eyes. On the edge of sleep she glimpsed herself as a young girl leaping into a leaf pile that her father and she had raked up in their maple-shaded back yard.

"Don't you two bring that dust into the house when you're done," her mother had called to them. "You know I'm allergic. Brush off your clothes and be sure you rinse your hands and face with the hose."

At the next session with her current therapist, a middle-aged woman addicted to spiked hair and multiple beads and bangles, Mel knew she would be urged to relate how the visit with her mother had gone. *Oh, fine,* Mel could tell her. *We slept together.*

Although to the best of her knowledge, Mel was her parents' legitimate daughter, it was hard for her to imagine her mother ever having sex. Except, unless Mel was adopted, just the one time when she was conceived. Or maybe she had it all wrong and they had humped like bunnies until Mel came along, after which disaster they used condoms or just abstained. Mel knew for a fact they had slept in separate beds ever since she could remember. "Because your father snores so," her mother said when Mel had the gall to ask about it, "and I am *such* a light sleeper."

Or maybe, as her mother claimed, it was true that Mel was such a difficult birth it nearly killed both mother and child. Which was why, her mother explained, Melissa should understand it did no good to keep begging for a little brother or sister. Her mother's female trouble kept her from ever having another baby. Melissa was an only child and that was it.

Her father never said anything about Mel's birth, except that he was happy to have been given such a brainy daughter. Until her wild teens that is, when Mel came to believe that having sex with lots of boys meant you were a popular girl and not, as she had realized too late, just an easy lay.

Christ, she was dying for a Scotch and soda. But no. No, she had 41 days going for her this time and would hate to let down her sponsor yet again. The woman had stuck by Mel for over a year, refusing to give up on her despite the repeated falls off the wagon. Louise was like a mother to Mel, people said, but Mel knew better. Louise was supportive and forgiving, and she seemed to actually *like* Mel.

"Mom," she said, "do you hear me? You still can hear, can't you?"

Was that a flicker of response on her face?

Mel again took hold of her mother's hand, squeezed it and felt what she thought was a twitch of response. Maybe, maybe not. After a while she let go. "Okay," she said, "if you just want to sleep, okay. You go ahead and I'll sit with you a while."

A piercing cat-like wail came from another room. Mel shivered. It sounded like someone's heart breaking, like a cry from hell.

She got up and closed the door. *How can anyone stand to be here?*

"Mom," she said, raising her voice in an effort to drown out the sound of suffering, "do you remember that stray cat I snuck into the house? Bitsy? And you said it had to go, but then you were the one it rubbed up against and it always picked your lap to sit on and so we got to keep it? What a sweet kitty, Bitsy."

Nothing from her mother.

Mel let her head hang down but fought to keep her eyes open. Christ, look at her own legs—dried out by the sun and wrinkled as lizard skin.

Why in hell did she make the effort to visit when all it seemed to do was cause pain for them both? The last time Mel was here, three years ago, it was another horror story. Her mother had spoken like a slut, fuck this, fuck that, and, slyly smiling, told Mel about the young black orderly who "serviced" his women patients when no one else was around. "My Lord," she said, "he's so *big* he fills you up until you think you'll burst!"

Mel immediately had gone to the nursing home administrator to demand action, but was assured there was no such orderly on staff and that nothing like that had ever happened except in Ruth's mind. She had lost her grip on reality and believed her dreams were real.

Which, when Mel had calmed down, she felt she could understand. In her teens she too had believed dreams were real. Like having sex with lots of boys meant you were popular and not just an easy lay.

Mel, too exhausted to carry on a one way mock conversation, dug her cell from her purse, turned up the volume and began playing the tunes she had recorded from Ruth's favorite oldies FM station.

On a previous visit, although her mother didn't recognize her, Mel discovered that she still knew all the lyrics to her favorite tunes and loved listening to singers like sweet Patti Page, weepy Johnny Ray and the syrupy crooner Bing Crosby.

One of Mel's rare happy childhood memories was hearing her mother in her girlish off-key voice sing along with the radio. As long as she believed no one was listening.

Would you like to swing on a star, carry moonbeams home in a jar ...

At the sound of Crosby's voice, her mother opened her eyes and mumbled something Mel couldn't make out.

Or be just the same as you are ...

Her mother groaned and slapped a hand down hard on the bed. "No."

"Mom. What's wrong?"

Or would you rather be a mule?

"No!"

Mel clicked off her cell just as a caregiver rushed into the room and asked her to stop, no music, please not play it.

"Okay," Mel said. "It's off, okay. But what's the problem?"

"Mrs. Michaels no more like the music. It make her cry and not to sleep."

"Well, I hope you know that I didn't mean to upset Mom. I was only been trying to comfort her. Really."

"Yes. I know this. Before, she like the music, Ruth does. But now, no, she cries and cannot sleep."

"Okay, okay,"

"But Mrs. Michaels still know her prayers and enjoy saying them."

"Oh, really."

The woman took a pearly, big-beaded rosary from the night stand and put it in her patient's hand. Immediately Mel's mother kissed the crucifix and began rasping "Our Father, who art in heaven ..."

The caregiver told Mel that sometimes one or two of the other patients came in to pray with Mrs. Michaels.

Mel nodded.

"She enjoy having people pray with her."

Mel raised a hand, palm flat to the woman. She'd heard the words. The woman was free to leave.

Without another look at Mel, the woman ran a damp cloth over her charge's face, tidied the covers and left.

So now Mel was heartless? Because she wouldn't say a lot of mumbo jumbo she'd never believed in? She had nothing but bitter memories of kneeling in church, praying by rote. "Oh, we are so unworthy; please forgive our sins, oh please save our souls ..." It was enough to make anyone with a functioning brain puke. By her early teens, she had seen through the shell game the Catholic Church played to rob you of your independence. Damn you to hell with original sin, then offer you redemption through slavish devotion to its rituals: baptism, confirmation, confession and communion. Like coke, it hollowed you out while promising you relief for your emptiness.

Ruth began counting her beads. "Hail Mary, full of grace." Then she looked at Mel as if just noticing her presence. "Oh, Missy," she said. "I didn't know you were here. Good girl. We can pray together."

"Mom, no," Mel said. "It's Mel."

"Yes. Then we can go shopping for your confirmation dress."

"*Melissa*, Mom. I'm all grown up."

"You'll look beautiful in it," her mother said. "All in white like a little bride. Now, where we were? Oh yes. Our father who art in Heaven ... Missy? Cat got your tongue? Who art in Heaven ..."

"... hallowed be thy name," Mel said in unison with her mother. "Thy kingdom come, Thy will be done ..." Then she stopped. She just could not repeat the old self-hating prayers. She was *not* an empty vessel waiting to be filled. Not anymore.

"... on earth as it is in heaven," her mother said.

Mel bit her tongue.

"Come on, sweetie. *Please.* Give us this day ..."

"God grant me the serenity," Mel whispered.

Her mother nodded, smiling. "... our daily bread, and forgive us our trespassers ..."

"to accept the things I cannot change"

"as we forgive those who trespass against us and"

"courage to change the things I can"

"lead us not into temptation but deliver us from evil"

"and the wisdom to know the difference."

"Amen," they said together.

ABOUT THE AUTHOR

Robert Flanagan was born in Toledo, Ohio, where he once worked as a dishwasher, night watchman, and janitor. He served in the U.S. Marine Corps Reserve, and graduated from the Universities of Toledo and Chicago. For three decades he taught at Ohio Wesleyan University and is a poet (*Reply to an Eviction Notice*), playwright (*Jupus Redeye*), as well as a short story writer (*Naked to Naked Goes* and *Loving Power*) and a novelist. His forthcoming novel *Champions* is set in Toledo's hard luck world of boxers and comics. A lifelong boxing fan, he earned his detached retinas sparring in local gyms. He lives with his wife Katy in Delaware, Ohio.

RECENT BOOKS BY BOTTOM DOG PRESS

BOOKS IN THE HARMONY SERIES
Stolen Child: A Novel
By Suzanne Kelly, 338 pgs. $18
The Canary : A Novel
By Michael Loyd Gray, 196 pgs. $18
On the Flyleaf: Poems
By Herbert Woodward Martin, 106 pgs. $16
The Harmonist at Nightfall: Poems of Indiana
By Shari Wagner, 114 pgs. $16
Painting Bridges: A Novel
By Patricia Averbach, 234 pgs. $18
Ariadne & Other Poems
By Ingrid Swanberg, 120 pgs. $16
The Search for the Reason Why: New and Selected Poems
By Tom Kryss, 192 pgs. $16
Kenneth Patchen: Rebel Poet in America
By Larry Smith, Revised 2nd Edition, 326 pgs. Cloth $28
Selected Correspondence of Kenneth Patchen,
Edited with introduction by Allen Frost, Paper $18/ Cloth $28
Awash with Roses: Collected Love Poems of Kenneth Patchen
Eds. Laura Smith and Larry Smith
With introduction by Larry Smith, 200 pgs. $16

HARMONY COLLECTIONS AND ANTHOLOGIES
d.a.levy and the mimeograph revolution
Eds. Ingrid Swanberg and Larry Smith, 276 pgs. $20
Come Together: Imagine Peace
Eds. Ann Smith, Larry Smith, Philip Metres, 204 pgs. $16
Evensong: Contemporary American Poets on Spirituality
Eds. Gerry LaFemina and Chad Prevost, 240 pgs. $16
America Zen: A Gathering of Poets
Eds. Ray McNiece and Larry Smith, 224 pgs. $16
Family Matters: Poems of Our Families
Eds. Ann Smith and Larry Smith, 232 pgs. $16

Bottom Dog Press, Inc.
PO Box 425/ Huron, Ohio 44839
Order Online at:
http://smithdocs.net/BirdDogy/BirdDogPage.html

RECENT BOOKS BY BOTTOM DOG PRESS

BOOKS IN THE WORKING LIVES SERIES
Story Hour & Other Stories
By Robert Flanagan, 122 pgs. $16
Sky Under the Roof: Poems
By Hilda Downer, 126 pgs. $16
Breathing the West: Great Basin Poems
By Liane Ellison Norman, 80 pgs. $16
Smoke: Poems By Jeanne Bryner, 96 pgs. $16
Maggot : A Novel By Robert Flanagan, 262 pgs. $18
Broken Collar: A Novel By Ron Mitchell, 234 pgs. $18
American Poet: A Novel
By Jeff Vande Zande, 200 pgs. $18
The Pattern Maker's Daughter: Poems
By Sandee Gertz Umbach, 90 pages $16
The Way-Back Room: Memoir of a Detroit Childhood
By Mary Minock, 216 pgs. $18
The Free Farm: A Novel By Larry Smith, 306 pgs. $18
Sinners of Sanction County: Stories
By Charles Dodd White, 160 pgs. $17
Learning How: Stories, Yarns & Tales
By Richard Hague, 216 pgs. $18
Strangers in America: A Novel
By Erika Meyers, 140 pgs. $16
Riders on the Storm: A Novel
By Susan Streeter Carpenter, 404 pgs. $18
The Long River Home: A Novel
By Larry Smith, 230 pgs. Paper $16/ Cloth $22
Landscape with Fragmented Figures: A Novel
By Jeff Vande Zande, 232 pgs. $16
The Big Book of Daniel: Collected Poems
By Daniel Thompson, 340 pgs. Paper $18/ Cloth $22;
Reply to an Eviction Notice: Poems
By Robert Flanagan, 100 pgs. $15
An Unmistakable Shade of Red & The Obama Chronicles
By Mary E. Weems, 80 pgs. $15
Our Way of Life: Poems By Ray McNiece, 128 pgs. $15

Bottom Dog Press, Inc.
PO Box 425/ Huron, Ohio 44839
Order Online at:
http://smithdocs.net/BirdDogy/BirdDogPage.html

Booboo Roi

A Murdered Murderer Too Soon: Royalty in 19TH Century Poland

(An Historical Tragedy, Set Forth as Plain Dramatic Reality A Step Out of Time)

MARVIN COHEN

Set in Janson Text with LaTeX.

ISBN: 978-1-952386-09-1 (paperback)
Library of Congress Control Number: 2021942455

Sagging Meniscus Press
Montclair, New Jersey
saggingmeniscus.com